doorways

doorways

MH SALTER

DAYTIME MOON PUBLISHING

Doorways is a work of fiction. Names, characters, places, and incidents either are the product of the author's imagination or are used fictitiously. Any resemblance to actual persons, living or dead, events, or locales is entirely coincidental.

Unless otherwise stated, all stories copyright © 2014 by MH Salter

The Inconstant Moon copyright © 2010 by MH Salter and Brett Cranswick

Excerpt from the novel *Dove – The Freedom Series Book One* copyright © 2014 by MH Salter

Excerpt from the novel *A Rose By Any Other Name* copyright © 2014 by MH Salter

Cover design by James, GoOnWrite.com

eBook ISBN: 978-0-9925267-0-2

Print Edition ISBN: 978-0-9925267-1-9

First published 2014 by Daytime Moon Publishing

Edited by Daytime Moon Publishing

All rights reserved

contents

Also by MH Salter — vii

About the Author — ix

About the Stories — xi

Dedication — xiii

Epigraph — xv

Frozen Souls — 1

The Weed And The Rose — 17

Oh, Brother — 21

The Inconstant Moon — 45

Sunrise Lake — 57

One More Glass — 63

The Other Side Of The Mirror — 73

The Saving Grace — 91

My Mother's Daughter — 105

Dove — 119

A Rose By Any Other Name — 133

Also by MH Salter

Dove – The Freedom Series: Book One
A Rose By Any Other Name

About MH Salter

Melanie Hyland Salter is the author of the popular *Freedom Series*, with the first instalment, *Dove*, being shortlisted for the Impress Prize for New Writers 2013.

Her fast-paced fiction, and high-tension plotlines play with imagery, metaphor, and poetic rhythm to create passages that flashbulb in the reader's mind, while her moral themes encourage readers to question the way they live and appreciate what they have.

The short stories in this anthology have won first prize, been published in Dark Edifice, and were Highly Commended by the Australian Community Writers Inc and NYC Midnight's Short Story Challenge 2014.

Melanie holds a BA in Writing, and a Diploma of Professional Writing. With a loving husband, who happily takes care of the household so she can write, Melanie lives in Adelaide with her three kids, two dogs, an army of cats, and a sheep named Harry Potter.

Please contact the author at:

mhsalter@daytimemoon.com.au or www.mhsalter.com

About the Stories

Frozen Souls (initially titled *Mountain Man)* was written for the television series Twisted Tales. Under the original title, it was published in *Dark Edifice Vol II* and Highly Commended by the Australian Community Writers Inc.

The Other Side of the Mirror was written for the television series, Twisted Tales.

The Saving Grace was Highly Commended in the NYC Midnight Short Story Challenge 2014.

Sunrise Lake won First Prize in the Away With Words 2008 Short Story Competition, and was published in the subsequent anthology.

One More Glass received a High Distinction from Deakin University.

My Mother's Daughter received a High Distinction from Southern Cross University.

The Inconstant Moon received a High Distinction from Southern Cross University, and contains poetic prose written by Brett Cranswick.

To Sally (my sister by default) as promised.

If the doors of perception were cleansed every thing would appear to man as it is, infinite.

    ~ William Blake, The Marriage of Heaven and Hell

frozen souls

Sam was freezing to death. The snow seeped through his heavy boots and layers of socks, into his skin, into his muscle, into his bone. At first his feet burned from the cold, now though, he felt nothing – which scared him more than the initial coldness.

He blew hot air into his cupped hands, shoved them under his armpits, and squinted at the white nothing ahead, at the white nothing behind, at the white nothing everywhere.

Is this what happened to the others? he thought. Is this what happened to Jules?

The mountain sighed in response; the breath of mist around him cleared.

And he let out a short laugh of disbelief.

In the distance shimmered a small wood cabin. It swayed and blurred in his vision.

Not real, he told himself.

Not real, as he stumbled up the path.

Not real, as his knuckles pounded wood.

And not real, as two wide eyes mooned out at him from the opening crack in the doorway.

'Good Lord, boy; you'll catch your death out there!' Stooped over and age-shriveled, his fat face hidden behind a white beard, an old man reached out and pulled Sam across the threshold. 'Quickly. Quickly!'

He shoved Sam into a pale leather armchair in front of a blazing fireplace, and then tucked a blanket over him. 'There now. How's that?'

Sam nodded, pulling the warm blanket tighter about his shoulders. 'Thank you, Sir.' The words tripped over his numb lips.

'Oh, no needs to thank me boy. No needs at all.' The old man smiled. 'You hungry?'

Sam nodded again.

But the man had already shuffled to the kitchen and ladled steaming liquid into two large bowls. 'Hope you like stew, boy.'

'Right now, I th-think I could eat anything!'

The old man laughed and cut four slices of bread with a meat cleaver. 'That's good, considering my cooking!' He carried the bowls and the bread back to the heat of the fire. 'Here, get this into you.' As he sat on the floor, his old bones creaked and he groaned along with them.

Realizing he sat in the only chair – the only piece of furniture in the cabin besides a matching leather lamp, a bed, and a coat rack – Sam began to get up. 'Please, sit here.'

The old man held up a hand. 'Don't be silly, boy! It's not too often I get company here,' he said. 'Least I can do is be hospitable. Besides, you ain't well.'

'Well,' Sam relaxed, 'if you're sure?'

'Course I'm sure! Wouldn't have said it otherwise, would've I?'

'I guess not. Thank you for being so kind, Sir.'

'Stop with the thankings already; you'll give me a complex, you will! And what's with all this *Sir* talk. The name's Winslow.'

'I'm Sam.'

'Nice to meet you, Sam. Now, please, eat!'

Sam gulped the stew. The sweet vegetables melted on his tongue. And there was something else. Some kind of spice, perhaps.

'Careful, there! Careful,' said Winslow. 'It's very hot.'

Letting his scalded tongue rest, Sam held up his spoon. 'Interesting cutlery.'

'Thank you.' Winslow's face reddened with pride. 'I carved 'em myself, I did.'

'Wood?'

'Bone.'

Sam lifted the bowl and studied it. 'These, too?'

'Yup. Skulls, they are.'

'What animal are they from?'

'Depends on what came snooping 'round. Course I made them a few years back, 'fore my conscience got the better of me.'

Sam dunked some of the bread. 'Conscience?'

'Turned vegetarian, I did. It's different when you live in a city; meat comes from a supermarket, wrapped nicely in cling wrap and Styrofoam. But out here, well, you have to hack the meat off living, breathing things yourself. Not nice.'

'No, I can't imagine it would be,' said Sam swallowing his sloppy bread. 'Wow. This has got to be the best stew I've ever had! What's your secret?'

'If I tell you, I'll have to kill you.' Winslow winked and smiled. 'Seriously now, what the devil were you doing walking 'round out there in this weather?'

'My friend, Henry,' said Sam, raising the spoon again and sucking it dry. 'He fell at Rudolph Point; I think his ankle is broken. He's waiting for me to get help.'

Winslow frowned. 'Only help you'll find out this far is little old me.'

'You don't have a telephone, or a radio we could call someone in by?'

'No phones in these parts, and my radio's busted. Been meanin' to fix the darn thing. But why were you two out in this blizzard in the first place?'

Sam shook his head. 'It's a long story.'

'My favorite kind. You can tell me while I get ready.' Winslow grunted himself off the floor.

'Ready for what?'

'Well, someone has to go and rescue this friend of yours! He must be going mad from the pain!'

'But you can't go out there in this storm!'

'Any other suggestions?' Winslow's face crisped with seriousness. 'How long has he been out there?'

'About three hours.'

'It *might* not be too late,' grumbled the old man.

'No, he should be fine; I left all the supplies with him: the food and both the sleeping bags and–'

'That's not what I mean, Sam. Why did you come into these mountains? It was because of the stories wasn't it? You were curious about the ghosts? And the missing hikers? Just like all the damn others.'

'No, it's not like that. Not exactly.' Sam sighed. 'I had a fight with my girlfriend, Jules. I was an idiot. She came home with a tattoo on her... um... self. So, not only had some sleazy tattoo artist seen her body, she comes home with *my name* inked into her skin! I shouldn't have, but I freaked out. She said I was afraid of commitment, and ran out of the house. She comes hiking up these parts all the time when she needs to get away from life, but this time she didn't come back. That was a week ago.' Sam looked down into his bowl. 'They cancelled the search party yesterday, but I can't give up on Jules. I love her.'

'So, you do know about the ghosts?' whispered Winslow.

'Everyone in town knows the stories about the

missing hikers, and the haunted mountain. Scared the crap out of me, but not Jules. She was fascinated. Always wanted to know what happened to them.' Sam paused. 'And maybe she found out.'

Winslow shook his head and slipped an arm into his jacket. 'No. They ain't just stories. These mountains... these mountains are evil, Sam. They're haunted by spirits who don't want to be dead.'

'Don't want to be dead? What does that mean?'

'It means they're desperate to be among the living again, and they'll do anything to get there. I've seen it before. Seen it with my own eyes. These spirits need bodies to live inside. If you spend too long alone out there... well... it still may not be too late for your friend. But I'll have to hurry.'

Sam stood. 'I'm coming with you.'

'Don't be silly, boy. You're in bad enough shape as it is; you'd only slow me down. Or worse – act as bait! You're lucky they didn't already get to you. Only reason I knew you were safe was you were shivering. *They* don't shiver.'

'Won't they go after you?'

Winslow shook his head. 'They don't want me; this body is old. They prefer the young. The healthy.' Winslow opened the door to the icy wind. 'Rudolph Point, you said?'

Sam nodded and shrank back into the blanket as the icy fingers of air pried at his skin.

'I shouldn't be too long. It's about half an hour away in this weather. There's more stew and bread over there. And there's more wood for the fire over there.' He pointed to a wooden box beside the hearth. 'Don't let it die.'

Sam nodded again.

'And make sure you keep this door closed. They can't get in if the door is closed. And whatever you do; do not go outside. No matter what, or *who* you think you hear, do not go out there!' He slammed the door and was gone.

And so, with nothing else to do but wait, Sam finished his soup, lost the battle with his exhaustion, and slept.

Winslow still had not returned when Sam woke, hours later. Afternoon light filtered in through the grimy windows. The sun would set soon, and it would be dark.

Where are they? First Jules, then Henry, and now I've dragged some innocent old man into my problems.

Sam snatched one of the many coats that hung on the rack like shed skins, and he shrugged into it. As he opened the door, Winslow's warning blew through his mind, but he shielded himself from it. He had to go out there. He had no choice.

'I must be crazy,' he said as the cold, white arms of the blizzard enfolded him. Icy fists pummeled and mugged him of all the stored up heat he had collected from the fire.

In just a few steps, the cabin was no longer visible

behind him. The whiteness ahead stretched on for as long as the whiteness behind. Infinite. Perfect. Uninterrupted snow in all directions. Not even a footprint acned the face of winter; a fresh carpet was laid down every second and Sam's tracks were hidden discreetly underneath.

He walked and walked and soon his whole body swore at him. Again freezing, again exhausted, and again lost.

When he saw the trail, he hoped he was delusional. But there is just something about seeing blood, especially fresh blood, which sobers you instantly to reality.

Following it, he prayed it wouldn't disappear under a layer of pristine white, and he prayed that whomever this blood had come from, it wasn't Winslow or Henry or Jules.

The trail led Sam right back to the cabin. His heart sped with worry as he burst through the front door, startling Winslow, who was hunched in front of the fire, bandaging a bleeding arm.

The old man jumped and raised the barrel of a shotgun with shaking hands.

'Winslow, it's me!' said Sam.

'Sam? How do I know that's really you in there?'

'You just have to trust me, Sir.'

'Sir?' Winslow lowered the gun. 'Sorry, I thought they had gotten to you as well. Shut that door! Bolt it, quickly! He tried to kill me. Tried to cut me up, he did!

Look at this!' Winslow thrust his bandaged arm out toward Sam.

'Who did this?'

'Shut the damn door!'

Sam closed the door and slid the bolt in place. 'Who did that to you?'

'Who do you think? Your friend did it, that's who.'

Sam shook his head. 'No. No way. Henry would never do that; Henry would never hurt anyone.'

'Stupid boy! Don't you get it? He is not *Henry* anymore. *They* got to him, Sam. Got to him 'fore I could!' Winslow looked down at his arm and continued bandaging it. 'I'm sorry, but you're friend is dead.'

Sam slumped back against the door. With tear-stung eyes, he looked up at Winslow. 'This is all my fault.'

'Fault is not your problem at the moment, boy. Why the hell did you go out there? I told you to stay put!'

'I went looking for you. You'd been gone for so long; I was worried something had happened.'

'Let me explain somethin' to you.' Winslow walked over to where Sam stood, and pointed out the window. 'Those things out there: they're like sharks – they smell blood and they come from miles. That friend of yours, he was the blood. Once they smelled him, word spread there was fresh prey about. And then you go swimming out there in shark-infested waters, drawing 'em all back to our little boat. I'd bet my left arm they're circling right now, waiting for you.'

'Well, we're both safe if we're in here right? Meanwhile, that left arm that you just bet is bleeding pretty badly. Let me see. It might need stitches.'

Winslow pulled away. 'No, it's fine, really. Just a scratch.'

'So, what do we do now? We're stuck out here, aren't we?'

Winslow nodded slowly.

'Well, what about the radio? Maybe we could fix it somehow?' Sam walked over to where the dusty radio sat. He flipped the ON switch. A green light glowed.

'I already told you that don't work.' Winslow shuffled over and reached toward the radio.

Bang!

His arm froze, hovering over the switch. 'You hear that?' Winslow whispered.

'Yeah.' Sam swallowed. 'I hear that.'

'It's them.'

'Could just be a tree scraping the side of the cabin?'

'That's no tree, boy.'

Bang! Bang!

'What do we do?' whispered Sam. 'Can we just wait them out? Wait until they leave?'

Bang!

Winslow laughed and turned away from the radio. 'I have to go out there.'

'What?'

'It's your only chance.' He grabbed the rifle and headed for the door.

'Are you nuts! What the hell are you doing?'

'Listen, they've ganged up out there. These walls won't keep 'em out much longer. I'm old; I've lived my life, I have. Might be able to bargain with 'em to spare you. No sense in both of us being taken, is there?'

'Wait...'

But the door closed, and Winslow was gone.

'I'm sorry!' called Sam.

A loud crackle of static spewed from the radio and Sam cried out in surprise. He pressed the call button and spoke into the handset: 'Hello? Hello? My name is Sam, can anyone hear me? We need help out here, hello?'

Silence.

'DAMN IT!' He threw the useless handset down and walked around to the armchair, slumping into it. Darkness was sneaking in through the windows, wrapping its cold fingers around Sam's throat. He switched on the lamp and watched the skulking shadows retreat to the corners of the cabin.

Then, suddenly, a different voice reached out through the emptiness: 'I read you, Sam. What's the problem?'

Sam jumped up and ran to the radio.

The bloody thing worked! Why would Winslow lie?

As Sam reached for the handset, he saw a shadow on the cabin wall that stopped his arm, stopped his thoughts, stopped his heart. With his breath frozen in his throat, he ran his fingers over the blurred image on the wall, and then slowly turned to walk back to the lampshade, from where the image was projecting. A heart with a word tattooed in the center of it. A name. *His* name.

Sam doubled over, clutching his stomach as bile rushed up his throat and filled his mouth. Just in time he grabbed his empty stew bowl from the floor beside the armchair and emptied the contents of himself into it.

When he was no more than hollow skin, he wiped his eyes, and stared at the bowl.

'What animal are they from?'

'Depends on what came snooping round... The missing hikers... just like all the damn others.'

Sam threw the bowl as if it burned his hand. Undigested stew splattered the floor.

That's why Winslow lied about the radio, thought Sam. He doesn't want help to arrive; doesn't want me to leave. There are no ghosts in these mountains; the missing hikers were all murdered.

With dread, Sam looked up at the darkening shape of the window. 'Oh, no... Henry!'

A rifle shot cracked the air into shards of falling echoes.

Sam grabbed the meat cleaver from the kitchen – forcing himself not to think of what, or who, the heavy blade had been used on – and ran to the door just as

Winslow filled the entrance. More blood covered him now.

'It's all okay, Sam.' The old man smiled and nodded. 'I took care of everything, I did.'

'What have you done to them?'

'I made a deal and they said–'

'Cannibal!' Sam swung the cleaver. It whistled through the air. 'Murderer!'

Winslow jumped backward. 'What are you talking about?'

'You're sick. I know what you are.' Sam swung the cleaver again, this time slashing into the flesh of the cringing man's arm.

Dropping the rifle, Winslow cried out in pain. 'No, Sam! I was helping 'em, I was!' Winslow cowered in Sam's shadow, and backed away against the door. 'I... I was freeing 'em! I was savin' their souls! You don't understand...'

'Oh, I understand.' Sam grasped the cleaver tighter in his white-knuckled fury. 'You developed a conscience huh? Couldn't kill innocent animals anymore – but humans aren't innocent; is that it? Well *she* was innocent; Jules was innocent, but you killed her! And you used her skin to upholster you're goddamn lampshade!'

'Please understand; she wasn't Jules anymore. She was possessed, and when I killed her body, I freed her soul. You should be thanking me!'

'Shut up! Just shut up!'

'Sam?' Winslow gazed up at Sam, his eyes wide, begging. 'Please?'

The meat cleaver sliced through the old man's throat, then dropped to the floor. The metallic chime of blade against floorboards rang through the cabin, lingering like a death knell.

Winslow clamped his fat fingers on his neck to keep the blood from pouring out, and death from pouring in. His old eyes continued to plead at Sam until they glazed over and his body slumped.

As shock set in, Sam's knees buckled and he began to sob.

What do I do now? Jules is dead. Henry is dead. All because of me. What do I have left?

Sam looked over at the rifle.

No, he thought. Too easy; I deserve a slow, painful, death for what I have caused. I deserve to starve. Or freeze. Whichever comes first.

Sobbing as he slid Winslow's heavy body out of the doorway, Sam stepped out into the freezing winds and was surrounded by ghostly forms – hundreds of them – all reaching toward him, into him, until he was no longer Sam.

His soul was pounded down, down, down inside his skin to make room for all the others that ripped into his body, and he couldn't move. He couldn't scream. He couldn't breathe.

And now that Winslow was dead, there would be no one left to save him.

15

the weed and the
rose

Summer brings crisp heat, dirty browns and clouds of dust, to parch the landscape. Wind is a scorched voice; through cracked, desiccated lips, it begs for water. The storm's angry quench whips the earth like gnashing teeth, and thunder growls fierce, 'til the calming song of *Season Change* starts all four elements singing.

Autumn's gown, crackling in folds of orange and red, blankets sunburned earth. She dances and whirls to the beat of passing time, graceful as the wind. Sunsets become trapped inside leaves as, one by one, trees shed their clothing.

Then winter frost-gems cover naked limbs of trees like glitter on skin. Diamond ice pendants are sun catchers dangling from skeletal branches.

As the seasons pass, he watches as life unfolds, a circle not whole. He, a lonely weed, waits with patience and yearning, for companionship. Loneliness is cold when surrounded by such life and warm affection, and the springtime-melt cannot thaw the weed's chilled heart as colour bursts forth. Animals pair up; mating dances, lust, sex, birth; and the weed, alone. Plants flower and seed; bees hover and tickle and leave the weed alone. Man with fleshy hands, admiring blooming petals, leaves the weed alone.

The dawn sky washed pink, casts a rosy glow on weed. True beauty's revealed: a rose bush blooming alongside our lonely weed, who loses focus. Nothing else exists but one particular rose, tall among the rest, however the same. With her petals red, she smiles, and she steals his heart. One flower, so ripe, velvet petals of desire opening for him. He can't look away, he *won't* look away – for why? What else could there be?

'Oh, love,' says the weed, 'such a time I've been waiting, so long, and in doubt. But now you are here, and if you will permit me, I'll love you always. I now understand: my wait for you was so long, for you are unique.'

'Sweet weed,' says the rose. 'Wise and loving weed... *my* weed, have you seen the snow?'

'Why, yes,' says the weed, and he tells of white crystals, while she smiles, sighs.

As the dewdrops shine on leaves and stems, and petals glitter through their bush, the other roses gasp and whisper in shock at this blossoming love.

'You can do better – with such beauty unsurpassed – than love straggly weed!'

But the rose cares not; weed has seen the seasons pass, seen the winter frost.

So they spend their days together speaking of things the rose only dreams 'til a silver flash, a metal gleam of scissors, cuts their love apart. The weed stares in shock as his rose is snipped and plucked and taken from him. There is no farewell, no goodbye for our lovers, only wintry hearts.

On the windowsill of the human's house she sits, our rose, in a vase. Weed stares at his love held captive in cut crystal behind sheer curtains, while outside, he finds that no more beauty exists; the world has gone grey. The sunsets, once rich, once painted skies with colour, are dull and ugly. The sunlight, once warm, shines down on weed with cold rays, and icy glows.

And as the days pass, weed sees rose wilt, her stem droop, petals fall away.

Then the windowsill stands empty: no vase, no rose. And weed wilts as well.

Thick gloves on strong hands grasp weed at his base and pull. Weed does not hold on. Roots let go of earth, no longer needing water, just death, painlessness.

Compost smells of dirt, grass clippings, vegetable peels. Weed is thrown on top. There, all withered, dry, is his rose, her beauty gone, scent unlingering.

Nothing so lovely – has the weed seen – than his rose, wilted but waiting.

Nothing so wanted – has the rose felt – than her weed, now by her side.

No words are needed as each absorbs the other in silent wonder. And there they remain, growing weaker in body but strong in spirit. Then the warm air chills, one last winter frost is here to ruffle spring's skirt.

'Look, love...' says the weed, his voice just a breath of air. 'Can you see the snow?'

But rose is silent. She does not answer her weed, through weakness? Or death?

Snow flurries drift down, collecting the rose and weed's two souls together.

oh, brother

Miranda sat on the couch in a rigid heap: muscles tensed around a slumping soul. Rage bubbled through the curves and crevices of her body. She was anger grown so hot it evaporated her tears and burned away her sorrow.

'Where the *hell* is he!' Words squeezed through gritted teeth and clenched jaw. Her face ached in frustration and she covered it with shaking hands.

When did things get this way? she wondered.

She and James had never been the perfect couple. All relationships had highs and lows, but theirs had never oscillated up and down; after its initial high, it slowly rolled downhill, coming to rest in the rut in which they'd been lodged for years. She'd never even noticed the downhill slant beneath them until she looked backward and saw how far from the peak they had slipped.

She stood and paced the room, parting the curtains on every lap past the window.

Miranda was sick of being treated like she didn't

matter. Sick of him forgetting every birthday or anniversary or anything that meant something to her. She had woken that morning full of resolve that by the time the sun went down, she would no longer be James's girlfriend. It was over. Done. Bye, bye. But when the sentence had finally fallen from her lips, James had fallen at her feet, crying and begging and promising he would change. He reminded her how good they could be together, and of course, she had believed him. They made love, and Miranda started to feel good, happy, confident that this last chance would not be like all the other last chances she had given. That this time, promises would be kept.

'Do you want anything from the shops?' James had asked, kissing her forehead and sliding out of bed.

She'd smiled and shaken her head.

'I won't be long. You stay right there; don't move a muscle. Just think about what I'm going to do to you when I get back.' He winked, and Miranda had giggled.

That had been three hours ago.

Miranda snatched up her car keys. She needed to vent. If she kept this all bottled up for much longer, she was going to smash something. Something of *his*, probably. She needed someone to talk to, someone who understood how she was feeling, someone to lend a sympathetic shoulder.

When she pulled into Dean's shady driveway, Miranda told herself she was there because he'd understand; after all, who knew James better than his very own brother. But when Dean appeared behind the gauzy fly screen of the security door and Miranda saw him smile in that way he only did with her, she knew her justifications had been nothing but flimsy excuses. She wanted to see him. Simple.

'Mira!' He opened the door and stepped back, combing his fingers through wet, messy hair. A thin cotton robe clung like a lover to his body and revealed every muscle. 'Come on in.'

The mixed scent of shampoo and the aftershave she'd bought him for Christmas ran its aromatic fingertips over her face as she passed by; her stomach fluttered and her head clouded.

Had he lingered in the doorway just enough to make her brush against him?

'You want a coffee or something?' he asked.

Something, she thought. 'Yes, please.'

She followed him into the kitchen, dropped her keys on the bench, and took a seat, grateful she now had something to hold her up.

I shouldn't have come. Especially not in this reckless mood. Just get up and walk to the car without even saying goodbye: that's what I should do.

'Milk and no sugar, right?'

'Right.' She laughed.

'What's funny?' He smiled that smile again as he took down two cups.

'After six years, James still doesn't know how I take my coffee.'

Dean shrugged. 'It's easy to remember: you don't need sugar because you're sweet enough already.'

Now, why can't James say things like that to me?

Dean placed a steaming mug on the bench in front of Miranda. As he leaned forward, cupping his hands around his own mug and resting on his elbows, his robe gaped open.

When Miranda realized she was staring at his chest, she quickly looked down into her coffee, but a second later, was again fixated on the tanned, firm muscles, which were within stroking distance of her fingers.

If I just lean forward over the countertop, like he is, I will be close enough to kiss him.

'I should go.' She stood up and stepped away from the bench.

'Wait. Don't. Something's bothering you, Mira. You know you can always talk to me.'

She sighed and met his eyes – so much like James's, but so completely different at the same time.

'It's my damn brother again, isn't it?' Dean came around the bench and placed his hands on her shoulders. His aroma once again ran its soft fingertips along every inch of her exposed skin until the tiny hairs on her arms started to rise. 'You deserve so much better than him, Mira. You deserve someone who treats you right, someone who loves you more than he loves himself.'

'James isn't that bad,' she whispered. 'He loves me…'

'Not like I…' Dean paused and cleared his throat. 'Not like I think he should.'

Miranda stepped away. 'I should go.'

Dean sighed, and nodded. 'Yeah. It's probably best.'

Outside, Miranda leaned back against the car and dropped her face in her hands. The tears snuck up on her, caught her off guard, and soon she was sobbing.

What am I doing? Of all the places to come, of all the people to see…

Would it really be that bad if I kissed Dean?

Of course it would! She scolded herself; it's terrible to even think it.

Terrible. Terrible. Terrible.

'Mira?'

She looked up.

Dean walked toward her.

Swearing softly, she wiped her face with her sleeve and wished she were a more attractive crier.

'You forgot these.' He jangled her keys, and when she reached up to take them, he grabbed her hand. Without speaking, he held her tear-soaked fingers in his. He tilted her chin up and looked into her soul. 'Are you sure you don't want that coffee?'

It was the kind of question that created a fork of existence in a parallel world.

*

'Are you sure you don't want that coffee?'

Her body answered before her mind had a chance; her feet lifted her upwards, her lips found his, and her tongue tasted the forbidden fruit it had craved for so many years. His kiss was soft, gentle, but with an underlying hunger that waited to pounce and devour her. She felt his teeth grasp her bottom lip gently; he was holding back, and the anticipation of what would happen when he finally let go made Miranda shiver.

Dean opened his mouth a little wider, drawing her deeper into the kiss. His hands let go of hers and he wrapped his arms around her, pulling her against him so closely she could feel the hardness of his chest against her breasts, could feel the pounding of his heart beating as rapidly as her own.

He drew away, panting. Their exhalations, hot and fast, joined together in the space between their mouths to form one shared breath.

She linked her hands behind his neck, pulling him toward her again. This time, the kiss was laced with a heat that threatened to ignite and consume them both.

The sound of the day – tires rolling, trees swaying, dogs barking – elbowed its way between them, and Miranda realized where she was. And that anyone could see them.

Dean blinked at the street as well, as if he too had forgotten they stood in his driveway. He swooped, lifted her in his arms, and carried her like a groom carries his bride through the front door and into the bedroom.

The satin sheets were strewn atop the mattress. As Dean laid her down amidst their slinky folds, Miranda could smell him within every fibre: sweet and musky. She inhaled him and felt her head stumble drunkenly from the fumes.

The weight of him pressed atop her. She slid her hands under his robe and traced the smooth skin of his back, along the crevice of his spine, he groaned her name in her ear.

As he undid her blouse buttons one by one, his lips nibbled her earlobe and then kissed along her neck. She closed her eyes, blocking out all visual distraction. Nothing existed now, but the feel of his tongue on her collarbone, his fingers stroking her nipples, the heat of his breath on her skin, and the smell of his body that wrapped so completely around her.

Is this really happening? If I open my eyes, will it be James, not Dean, whose mouth is kissing my belly-button right now? Or is it just another fantasy? Another daydream? God, I hope I never wake!

Dean's lips ventured lower and lower; his teeth popped open the button of her jeans. He slid them down over her hips and ran his tongue slowly across the lace of her underpants.

'No!' Pulling him up, level with her, she finally opened her eyes to see his beautiful face inches from hers. She sucked in a breath of wonderful shock that, yes, this was really happening.

'No?' He frowned.

Wriggling under him, she kicked off her jeans and slid out of her underwear. 'I just want you inside me. I don't want anything else but that.' She untied his robe and pulled him down onto her.

He was pressing hard against her, and she wrapped her legs around his middle to guide him.

For a fraction of a second she heard the voice of guilt screaming out her name, and for a fraction of a second she wondered if she had made the right choice by starting that blissful kiss on the front lawn.

But then she felt the pressure of him slide inside her, heard him groan, felt him shudder, and she forgot about any other possible outcome that a different decision might have created.

*

'Are you sure you don't want that coffee?'

Shivering on the front lawn, she closed her eyes and broke the spell of Dean's gaze. And with the link between them broken, she pulled her hand from his and turned away.

If I can keep my back to him, I'll be fine.

She felt him move; the air molecules around her suddenly seemed less frantic now that he was out of her personal space.

'I'm sorry,' said Dean.

'Me, too,' she whispered as she opened the car door and slid inside. Sorrier than you can possibly know.

She kept her eyes straight ahead as she backed out the driveway and sped away from temptation. For a fraction of a second she wondered if she was making the right choice by leaving Dean standing on the front lawn, the lean plains and taut muscles of his naked body all too visible beneath his thin robe. For a fraction of a second she let herself imagine how amazing it would be. But she knew it was wrong. Perhaps that was why it was so damn appealing.

She drove aimlessly. Bypassing all detours in her mind that would lead her back to Dean, Miranda let her thoughts unwind and ravel off behind her. She'd given a huge chunk of her life to James; she had to admit that he was special, she'd been aware of it from their very first kiss. He had the ability to make her feel like the only person in the world – when he wanted to. But he also had the ability to drive her insane with neglect.

This morning, he'd reminded her things weren't that bad after all, and they had the potential to be great. And she wanted great. What woman didn't? When they had made love she knew just how much she needed him in her life. How much she wanted him.

And then he had vanished – like he always seemed to do – and her anger had replaced him.

Why can't he show me some God damned respect? She punched the steering wheel. She was sick of it. She was really sick of it. As much as she loved him, she deserved to be treated right, like Dean had said.

Shaking her head, she tried not to let her thoughts wander back to Dean and his exposed chest and his invitation to return inside.

As she pulled into her driveway, Miranda saw James's car parked under the carport. A fresh wave of anger swelled inside her, thankfully burning away all feelings of forbidden lust toward her boyfriend's brother.

She stomped up the path. The front door was open and she stormed through, ready for a fight; the words 'Where the hell were you?' ready to pounce from her lips and rip out his throat. But what she saw froze her. Her anger vanished. Shock crept icily through her veins.

'James?' she whispered. 'Oh my God.'

A loud bang echoed around the room, and Miranda covered her gaping mouth with a shaking hand.

*

After they satisfied the pent up feelings of lust that fermented for so many years, Miranda and Dean made love again, slowly, sensuously, perfectly.

Shadows crept into the room during the three hours they spent in bed, and in the orange light from the setting sun, Dean glowed.

'What happens now?' he asked. His head rested on Miranda's naked chest.

'What do you want to happen now?' she whispered.

'I want you to be happy.'

'Then I guess we stay in this bed forever, because right now I'm happier than I've been in a long time.' She stroked his hair.

'I could handle staying with you forever,' he said, lifting his head and meeting her gaze.

'What about James?'

'I'll handle James.'

'Oh, God. This is so messy.' She felt hot tears burn her

eyelids. 'I shouldn't have done things this way! James doesn't deserve to be cheated on!'

'Mira, listen to me.'

'I'm a horrible person!' she sobbed.

'Mira!'

Miranda slid out from under Dean, and began to dress. 'This is going to destroy him. Oh, what have I done?'

'What are you doing?'

'I have to go. I can't be with you until I end things with James.'

'No, don't leave.'

'I'm not a cheater, Dean! I don't want to be this person!'

'Miranda, he...' Dean ran a hand through his hair. 'James cheated on you!'

She stared at him. 'What?'

Dean licked his lips and took a breath. 'He begged me not to say anything.'

'When?' She sat. 'Who with?'

'Last year, at his office Christmas party. I caught him and his secretary doing it on the copy machine.'

'His secretary? Ugh, that's so cliché.'

'I'm sorry. He said he wanted to be the one to tell you. That's why I never said anything.'

'I can't believe he would do that to me!' Miranda stood to finish getting dressed, but collapsed onto the bed again, her sobs returning. 'What am I saying? Who am I to judge?'

'Hey, hey!' He stroked her face and kissed her cheeks dry.

'Take a breath. Look at me. Now I want you to concentrate on how you felt a minute ago, okay?'

'Okay.'

'Happy,' he said.

She nodded.

'Peaceful.'

She nodded again.

'And... in love?' This time it was said as a question and Miranda could hear the fear in his voice.

'Yes.' She smiled. 'In love.'

'Phew!' He laughed. 'All right, then. If you can put a sample of those feelings away somewhere inside you, all you'll have to do is get them out again when you feel life is getting too hard. And always remember that I'll be here for you.'

'When are we going to tell him?' she asked.

'I guess, the sooner the better. Get it over and done with.'

She nodded and felt the tears rising again.

Neither of them spoke in the car on the way to her house.

As she pulled into the drive, Miranda saw James's car in the driveway and a fresh wave of anger swelled inside her, thankfully burning away all feelings of guilt about what she and Dean had just done.

If he'd treated me with any kind of God damned respect, thought Miranda as she stomped up the path to the front door, then maybe I wouldn't have been driven into the bed of my boyfriend's brother!

The front door was open and she stormed through, ready for a fight; the words 'Where the hell were you?' ready to pounce *from her lips and rip out his throat. But what she saw froze her. Her anger vanished, and shock crept icily through her veins.*

'James?' she whispered. 'Oh my God.'

A loud bang echoed around the room, and Miranda covered her gaping mouth with a shaking hand.

*

The room overflowed with vases. Each vase overflowed with red roses. Lit candles covered the floor. In the middle of the room, in the center of the concentric circles of flowers and candle flames, sat James. A freshly-popped bottle of champagne in one hand, and a diamond ring in the other.

'Sorry I took so long, honey,' he said. 'It was so hard to choose the right one; I wanted it to be absolutely perfect for you, because you're absolutely perfect for me.'

'Oh, James.' Miranda took a step forward, then a step back.

'Marry me, babe?'

*

Miranda stepped into the lounge room, which was covered in shattered vases, shredded roses, and broken candles. Dry wax splattered the carpet and walls.

In the middle of the mess slouched James. An empty champagne bottle beside him, and a freshly-popped bottle in his hand.

'Where the hell were you!' he yelled at her.

'Me?' she yelled back. 'What about you!'

'Wouldn't you like to know, hey?'

'Ugh! You're drunk!' She walked forward and snatched the bottle from his grasp. 'I can't believe you, James. What happened to: I can change? You swore, no more drinking! Is that where you went then, was it? Down the pub as usual!'

'Well, where were you?' He stood up, and swayed on his feet. 'I've been waiting here for hours!'

'She was with me.' Dean stepped forward.

James stared for a second as if he'd only just realized someone else stood in the room.

'It's over, James,' said Miranda. 'I've had enough.'

'What?'

'I want you to move out.'

James's face flushed red, but he kept his voice low. 'Fine.' He looked at Dean. 'All right if I crash at your place for a while, man? The Misses and I seem to be going through a slight rough patch.'

'Um...' Dean cleared his throat and looked at Miranda, who nodded. 'I don't think that's a good idea, mate. Listen, Miranda and I have something to tell you.'

*

'Miranda?' said James.

'Huh?'

'Will you marry me?'

Her shock suddenly dissolved and allowed realization to flood her. Happiness followed the realization, and guilt followed the happiness. She'd been angry with him, she'd been planning to break up with him, she'd even considered sleeping with his brother! When all the while, he had been in a jewelry store picking out a diamond.

'I'm sorry, James.' She rushed across the room and flung her arms around his neck, pressing her face into his chest.

'You *won't* marry me?' he whispered into her hair.

'No, I mean, I'm sorry I was so angry with you!'

'Well, I'll forgive you if you put this ring on.' He touched her chin and tilted her face up to him. 'Be my wife, Miranda.'

A grin started at her lips and then spread throughout her entire body. 'I'd love to!'

Slipping the ring on Miranda's finger, James lifted her hand to his lips and kissed it, then carried her – like a groom carries his bride – to the bedroom.

The bed had been scattered with rose petals in the shape of a heart. Scented candles burned on the bedside table. James watched her, smiling, as Miranda's eyes widened and her newly glittering hand covered her mouth.

'It's beautiful,' she whispered.

'Not as beautiful as you.' He set her down. 'I know life with me hasn't been the one I promised to give you, but that changes now. I've been taking you for granted and I've been an idiot. You are my world, babe, and from this second forward I swear I'll make sure you know that, every damned day.' His lips were quivering with emotion as he pressed them against Miranda's. 'I must be the luckiest man in the world.'

She felt her cheeks become wet, and she pulled away from him. 'You're crying!'

'Yeah,' he smiled. 'Don't tell anyone.'

Miranda ran her hands up into James's hair and pulled his face down to hers. 'I'm the lucky one,' she said, to herself as well as him.

How could I have even considered being with Dean? How could I have been so blind? The whole time I've been wishing for someone perfect, he's been right in front of me!

James slipped Miranda's shirt up over her head, unbuttoned her jeans, and slid his hand between her legs. He walked her backwards and together they fell onto the bed.

Miranda unbuckled James's belt, unzipped his fly, and let her fingers close around him. He hardened in her hand.

'Oh, Miranda, I love you so much,' he whispered.

'I love you too, Dean.'

James sat up. His face paled.

'What?' asked Miranda.

'You just said...' He moved away from her touch. 'You just said, "Dean".'

'What!' Miranda felt her face burn. 'That's... that's ridiculous.'

'Is it?' he asked. 'I knew you had a thing for him.'

'No, I don't!'

'Oh come on, Miranda, I've seen the way you behave around him. I *thought* it was just harmless flirting...'

'It is!' she said.

'So you admit it? You *do* have a thing for him.' James stood and pulled up his pants. 'I can't believe I wanted to marry you, when the whole time you were wishing I was my brother!'

*

'My own brother?' James's fists clenched at his sides. 'You're leaving me for him? I don't believe this!'

He surged forward. Dean puffed out his chest, ready to defend himself, but James just shouldered past, snatched his car keys off the wall peg and slammed the front door behind him.

Miranda sat shakily on the edge of the sofa. 'That went well.'

'He's not going to drive is he?' Dean parted the curtains. 'He's had a whole bottle of champagne.'

James was already in his car, the engine roared angrily.

'No, he can't get out; my car is blocking him in.'

James's car revved again, louder, and he swerved through the flowerbed, onto the front lawn, around Miranda's car, and out into the darkening street.

'Oh, shit!' said Dean.

*

'Where are you going?' called Miranda, buttoning her shirt and following James out of the bedroom. He paused in the hallway as if about to speak, but then shook his head, grabbed Miranda's car keys and stormed out the front door.

'Shit,' she muttered, as he drove away in her car.

In the kitchen, she called his mobile, but heard it ringing from the lounge. 'Damn!' She slammed the phone receiver back in its cradle. All she could do was wait for him to calm down and come home. Then she'd have to explain. What was she going to say? That, yes, she'd had a crush on his brother for their entire relationship. That, yes, she often wished she'd stood next to Dean, not James, that night at the bar. And that, yes, she always wondered how her life would be if Dean, not James, had bought her a drink and taken her home.

Hours morphed into shadows and flooded the room by the time the car pulled into the drive. As she walked down the hall, rehearsing her apology in her head, she frowned when she heard the doorbell.

James wouldn't ring the bell...

Miranda opened the door and felt her stomach roll when the man on the porch offered her a smile and a curt nod as he tucked his blue cap beneath his arm.

'Are you the spouse of Mr. James Byron?'

'Yes,' she whispered to the police officer.

'I'm sorry to be the one to inform you, but he has been involved in a car accident.'

*

'A car accident?' Miranda's hand rose to her mouth. She felt Dean's hands on her shoulders and she leaned back against his chest, grateful for the support.

'Is he all right?' Dean asked the policeman on the front porch.

'He's been taken to the hospital,' said the officer. 'Apparently he's having some trouble regaining consciousness.'

'But, he will be all right, won't he?' Miranda said.

The officer smiled sympathetically. 'Can I give you a ride?'

'No, I can take her,' said Dean. 'Thank you, officer.'

*

Miranda shook in the passenger seat of Dean's car. 'Thanks for picking me up.'

'Don't be silly,' he said. 'You shouldn't be driving in your state.'

'He will be all right, won't he?' she asked. It was a question that had been repeated a million times in her head.

'Of course,' said Dean, nodding. 'Of course.'

They arrived at the hospital and as they walked Dean put his arm around her shoulder. Miranda was grateful for this friendly gesture, and realized all she could feel in his touch now was friendship. There was no desire, no secret longing to have him press against her. Granted, that may have been because she was numb with shock and worry about James, but Miranda could tell her feelings for Dean were gone. All this time, she had sculpted Dean into everything she'd wanted James to be; she'd been too preoccupied thinking about what she didn't have to realize what she did have. And now she was being punished. Now, she might lose everything.

It was difficult to see James beneath all the tubes and wires that snaked over his body – a sight that throbbed Miranda's stomach with fear – but beneath them all she could see his chest rising and falling – a sight that stung her eyes with thankful tears.

She sat beside his bed and took his hand. Felt a soft squeeze. 'You're awake!' she sobbed.

'I'll just wait out here,' said Dean, backing into the hall.

'Miranda?' James whispered. His voice was husky and weak.

'Shh,' she said. 'Don't talk, I'm here, honey. I'm so sorry about before, I...'

'I need you to know something.'

'It's okay; you just need to rest now.' She smoothed the hair from his forehead and leaned down to press her lips on his skin.

'I cheated on you,' he said.

She froze and sat back to stare at him. 'What?'

James licked his lips and took a breath. 'Last year, at

the office Christmas party. I had a few too many and I ended up on the copy machine with Raelene.'

'Your secretary?'

'I'm so sorry; I've regretted it every day – that's why I haven't been treating you the way you deserve ...'

'Why? Because you screwed your secretary, I get punished?'

'I've felt so guilty; I didn't know how to tell you.' He reached for her hand but she pulled away from him. 'Please? Could you ever forgive me?'

'I can't believe you would do that to me!' Miranda stood. 'Why are you telling me now?'

'Because, when you said Dean's name earlier, I realized that maybe you were considering making the same mistake I did. It scared me.'

'You actually think I'd stoop so low as to screw your own brother!' Miranda wrenched the engagement ring from her finger.

'No, don't do that, please?'

'Go to hell, James!' Miranda threw the ring at him and ran from his room.

James rested his head back against the pillow and closed his eyes. He let out a deep sigh.

Then he started to buck and writhe as high-pitched beeps filled the room.

*

'Get the hell out of my room!' said James, as Miranda and Dean entered.

'You're awake!' said Miranda, rushing to his bedside.

'I'll just wait outside,' said Dean.

'You can get out, too,' James said, snatching his hand out of Miranda's grasp.

'Honey, I'm so sorry. I've made a terrible mistake, and I want to spend the rest of my life proving to you that we're meant to be together. I love you.'

'What about him?' James nodded to the doorway.

'I told you; that was a mistake. Dean and I both realize it now.' She held his hand again, and gripped tight when he tried to pull away. 'We all make mistakes, right? Aren't I entitled to one?'

He stared straight ahead, saying nothing.

'What!' She frowned at him. 'So, it's okay for you to screw someone else, but not me?'

James's mouth dropped. 'How do you...'

'Dean told me.'

'Course he did.'

'James, I almost lost you today, and it made me realize that if I did lose you, I'd lose myself. You're a part of me, I need you, and I know you need me.'

James rested his head back against the pillow and closed his eyes. He let out a deep sigh.

Then he started to buck and writhe as high-pitched beeps filled the room.

Blue material surged all around Miranda as doctors and nurses flowed into the room and washed her out the door.

*

'I'm so sorry,' said the doctor. 'We did all we could.'

Miranda sat in the waiting room in a rigid heap: muscles tensed around a slumping soul. She stared at the lime green walls.

Who the hell chose such a disgusting color? I mean, really, it's horrid! Is it supposed to be calming? Because it most definitely is not.

Then Dean put his arm around her shoulder, and she crumpled under its weight.

If only James turned onto the highway one minute earlier, one minute later, things might be different now. James might not be dead. Perhaps, somewhere in a parallel world, thought Miranda, he isn't.

*

'You can go in now,' said the doctor. 'He's weak, but he'll be all right.'

'You asshole!' said Miranda, as she entered James's room again. 'You gave me a God damned heart attack!'

'Well, you slept with my brother, so I guess we're even.' He smiled weakly up at her. 'Sorry,' he whispered. 'Listen.' He raised his hand, searching for hers, and she grasped it. 'Can we start over? Both of us? Clean slates?'

43

Miranda nodded and pressed his hand against her cheek; her throat choked closed on words she couldn't speak.

James nodded to the small cupboard in the corner of the room where his possessions had been stored. 'Get my jacket. Look in the inside pocket.'

Miranda stood and opened the closet door. She reached into his coat pocket and her fingers closed around a small velvet box.

the inconstant moon

The Girl's mobile beeps. SMS received.

The Boy's words: *Looks like a full moon tonight.* That sentence has her hugging herself to keep emotion from splitting her seams. For in his simple statement, wrapped in those six words, is me.

As this cold winter moon – wide as a shocked eye – stares down at the Girl and the Boy in their respective pockets of the world, I wonder if it remembers me. Remembers *us*. Remembers that first night after which every full moon became a marker of my longevity. For I am the Relationship these two people conceived, brought into the world, nurtured, cherished, and then discarded.

It began when the Girl sent the first timid email, to which the Boy replied, and each recognized in the other something for which they had been searching: he needed to be healed, she needed to heal him. And so, along with my gestation, their polite correspondences continued.

*

The Boy: *I want you to know that I'm a little bit crazy. But I think it will pass. It's really just developed in the last six months. I would like to return to a more optimistic frame of mind. You're welcome to try to influence me. I would like that.*

The Girl: *A little bit crazy huh? Well, aren't we all to some degree? Tell me something positive about yourself.*

The Boy: *I write sonnets. I'm also big on family. That's positive. I love my mum. And I tell her. I have great taste in shoes. I look after my teeth. When I'm not morbidly depressed. I can be mind-bendingly romantic... let me practise on you.*

*

By the time the first full moon shone down on us, witnessing their first physical meeting and my birth, they were both already secretly in love with me – in love with the idea of love.

'I'm not going to kiss you,' said the Girl, as she walked him out to his car. 'Because we're just friends, remember, and friends don't kiss each other.'

The Boy shrugged and smiled and stared up the stars. 'Would you do something for me? Would you sit on the boot of my car? There's something I want to do.'

'No kissing,' she warned.

'Trust me.'

And he helped her perch lightly on the edge of his green Renault, her legs in a V between which he stood.

Beneath the voyeuristic moon, he laced his fingers in her long hair, pressed his face against her neck, and inhaled her deeply. The heat of his breath on her skin made her shiver. He moved to the other side of her neck, lingered, moved back again. Then he dipped his head to the small hollow at the base of her neck where her pulse pounded beneath his lips.

As she trembled beneath his touch, she asked me, 'Am I going to fall in love with this man?'

Without hesitation I answered her. 'Yes. Oh my, yes.'

*

The Boy: *In case I die today, I'm going to pretend you already told me you love me. I have been waiting so long. I have despaired of you ever finding me. I need you like the air I breathe. You are my reason now. I want you to love me. Going to make it impossible for you not to love me. I want you to come to me, again and again, in every area of my life until there is nothing I am that is not you.*

The Girl: *...I think I'm falling in love with you.*

The Boy: *Don't worry, I'll catch you.*

*

The second full moon craned its pearly neck and squinted through the lace curtains of the Boy's bedroom window, where it watched us, all three, entangled and silent. Her finger traced the tattooed lines over his heart: the Japanese symbol for fortress. Her head rested on his chest so she didn't have to meet his eyes when she took a deep breath and finally said the words he'd been waiting to hear: 'I love you.'

Beneath her ear, his heart pounded out a proud victory. But he did not speak.

'Do you love *me?*' she asked.

Another long pause. She held her breath.

He finally replied: 'I *need* you.'

'That's not what I asked,' she said.

Again his pause. Again her held breath.

He tilted her chin up, forced her to look at him, and placed his fingers on her lips to silence her. 'I love you,' he whispered.

She smiled.

And I felt myself grow stronger.

*

The Girl: *I love you. I love you. I love you. To the moon and back, I love you.*

The Boy: O, *swear not by the moon, th' inconstant moon, that monthly changes in her circled orb, lest that thy love prove likewise variable. ~ Romeo and Juliet*

The Girl: *I love you!*

*

The third full moon silvered the warm sand and the cooling ocean and their goosebumped skin, dressed only in the silken threads of night and each other's touch.

His lips hovered above hers, teasing, brushing, and

pulling away when she tried to close the distance between them.

'You're my Goddess.' He shuddered beneath her as they rose and fell on the surface of the ocean. 'Let me worship you.'

Between them, their souls mingled and danced in clouds of white exhalations that lifted like prayers and disappeared into the ether.

*

The Girl: *To converse in form of only five-seven-five, accept the challenge?*

The Boy: *Send and I'll return, across the vast wilderness, haiku mating calls.*

The Girl: *A whisper of leaves calls the past to the present: your breath in my ear.*

The Boy: *My thoughts fly to you. We meet among cirrus clouds and fall to the earth.*

The Girl: *Locked inside your heart. It's cold in here without you. When will you join me?*

*

The fourth moon was blue. This moon lingered, refusing to move on in case everything was different when it returned. This moon, bright as hope, saw the Boy and the Girl separated by a job lost, a town left behind, a search undertaken, a desire for success. This moon kept them joined as they stood apart. This moon had them gazing with tearful eyes at the same sky, at the same moment, each imagining the other imagining them imagining the other...

*

The Girl: *Don't you think it's a little bit of a coinkydink that, after you meet and fall hopelessly in love with a girl who lives in a town a million miles away, your world suddenly dissolves providing you with the perfect opportunity to now merge your life with hers? Maybe it's all meant to be.*

The Boy: *Whatever. A million miles away. Travelling through country by train; coming up to the new town soon. Used to say I had the best job in the world when I was in the other place. Can't believe how lucky I am and how close I came to throwing away all hope of professional development. Wanna make the absolute best of this gig if I get it.*

*

The fifth moon illuminated new beginnings. A new life. A new job. A new town. A new challenge. A new focus. A new order of importance.

The fifth moon illuminated me in a way nothing else could. It alone had the power to reveal how I had weakened: the way my clothes hung off my frame, the way my skin – white as fear – stretched taut over bones that were pressing so forcefully outward, needing to escape, producing shadows like the blade on a sundial. I was malnourished and hallucinating and shivering in the corner.

The fifth moon illuminated the beginning of the end.

*

The Girl: *Hi there, don't know if you remember me, but I'm the girl you're in love with...? Okay, I understand that you've started a new job that may be swamping you, but it only takes a couple of minutes to send a quick email. In my opinion, even feeling totally swamped by work isn't an excuse to act in a manner that you know will be hurtful to me!*

The Boy: *Oh sure, I remember you. You're the chick who keeps telling me maybe you don't want a relationship and then gets all girly over the fact that I might have other priorities. Hope you're okay, all things considered.*

*

The sixth full moon was a bloody stain in the sky. A Luna eclipse. A luminous body cast in shadow by the very object around which it gravitated. Beauty concealed by the very thing it loved.

*

The Boy: *You sound like you want me to worship and idolise you.*

The Girl: *Of course I want you to worship and idolise me: that's how you should feel when you love someone. It's how I have always felt about you. That's what love is.*

The Boy: *I don't know what love is. I don't think I believe in love.*

The Girl: *But... all this time you've been telling me you love me...*

The Boy: *Because I hope that one day I will. I respect you. I rely on you. I need you.*

The Girl: *Love is the inability to imagine your life without the other person in it. You seem to be able to do this quite easily.*

*

The seventh moon was pale with impatience and morbid curiosity. It sneaked across the blue sky at noon, like the curious who roll by and stare into the wreckage of a fatal car crash. The Girl and the Boy had met on a grassy hill overlooking the town that was the midpoint of their shared long-distance. The Boy folded on the grass and looked up at the Girl as she sat on the bonnet of his car.

Above them, the clouds were pure white, as if all moisture had been siphoned from them by the Girl's eyes, which floated and bobbed in a sea of tears.

'I don't know how to heal from your words,' she said. 'I healed you when you needed it; now I need you. I need you to help me.'

His eternal silence was finally broken by a shake of the head, a sigh and an unfolding of the body. He stood between the V of her legs. 'I can't afford to take any focus off my work at the moment.'

Cupping his face, she sobbed. 'I don't know how to say goodbye to you.'

'Then *don't!*'

'I'm not going to be with somebody who doesn't love me.'

'This can't be the end,' he whispered.

'Why not?'

'Because I want you to *believe* I love you.'

And before she dissolved into nothing, the Girl pushed away from his chest, ran to her car, and sped away from him. From me. From us.

*

The Girl: *It hurts because I lost my future. It hurts because I have lost my present. It hurts because the past is full of good memories that bring pain, and bad memories that also bring pain. Can't win.*

The Boy: *I know you're struggling. I feel so useless, ambivalent. I can't hold down this job and be there for you at the same time. If I give up the job, I won't be the same person and I will throw in the relationship. Equally if I throw in the relationship, I don't think I can keep myself together to hold down a responsible job.*

The Girl: *I think you have stolen my soul. It doesn't even feel as if I've lost half of myself. It's all gone. I don't know who I am now. I don't recognise this person, this face in the mirror with the fake smile and the irises tinged blue from tears.*

*

The eighth moon could no longer see the Boy or the Girl as each had become so shrouded in shadow, had fallen so far within the shells of their own bodies, they were only visible if you peered down the well of their eyes with a strong torch and shouted their names into the cavernous emptiness that had become them.

And me? Well, I was casting that aforementioned shadow that enshrouded.

I was that deep well of emptiness that entrapped.

I was pure longing personified.

I was Hell.

*

The Boy: *Rocking gently, seeping hot salty tears, occasionally heaving under the breath of exhaustion, this shattered frame entangled in itself, this weightless form of insubstantial shape, stirring in the path of oncoming tumultuous emotions, prepares to be jettisoned into an ocean of neglect, to vanish under a bare windblown ripple. Wave upon wave of sorrow wash fragments of you ashore. I collect you like driftwood, lashing together what's left, otherwise stranded upon the island of my heart, wondering if this is the answer to my message in the bottle. I could die here. Wouldn't I die trying to risk the vast ocean anyway?*

The Girl: *Some say the body and soul are two separate things. That they are not really connected. But if this is true then why, when the soul is struck, does the pain of that blow roll through the body in a forceful wave of physical agony? The stomach fists, clenches and cramps, and from that fierce and sharp ache it flows outward in concentric circles like ripples on the surface of a pond. It crashes across the chest, down the arms and legs; it closes the throat with a sob and fills the head with tears that are forced out in an attempt to flush away the pain, to carry it out of the body on a thin tide of salt water through the windows of the soul.*

*

The Girl presses the power button on her phone, and his words (*Looks like a full moon tonight*) vanish into blackness. She stands and draws aside the curtains of her room. The present full moon is hidden by thick cloud; she is unable to receive the illumination that shines down on the Boy. And as she thinks of him, she thinks of the different ways in which I am able to illuminate a life. For her, I was hot and bright as the sun; for him, I was relaxed and calm as the moon. But while the sun is able to generate its own radiance and heat, moonlight is simply a pale reflection of the sun.

She lies down and prays for dawn.

He lies down and prays for disconnection.

And I turn from them both and dissipate to the place where forgotten memories go to die. There, I'll await my reincarnation and a new moon.

sunrise lake

The sky shone ruby and gold over the lake. The water was clear glass, encasing the sunrise beneath. Gnarled, dead trees stretched their limbs through the mirrored surface, reaching for nothing. Slowly, the silence began to shatter, allowing sounds of morning to drip through its cracks: the flutter and shuffle of graceful black swans as they swam through the sky; the swish of the waking wind as it yawned through the reeds; the harmonious chorus of sparrows overhead as they sang *good morning* to the day.

Bill and Ebony enjoyed the tranquillity of the morning together. They sat side by side, not holding hands but leaning against one another, smiling up at the heavenly roof woven with shimmering threads of golden fire. It wasn't very often they had time to themselves, not since the triplets had arrived.

'We've been coming here every year for five years,'

said Ebony, 'and I swear the sunrise gets more breathtaking every time.'

Bill nodded. 'This place certainly has a magic to it.'

'Well, it must,' said Ebony. 'It brought me to you.'

Bill leaned over and gave Ebony a peck on the cheek. 'I love you, too.'

It was here Bill and Ebony had first met and fallen in love, on a morning just like this, with the sky a brilliant oil painting on the canvas of eternal possibility.

'Come on, we'd better get back.' Ebony stood and stretched. 'The kids will be waking soon and wanting breakfast.'

An innocent flash of light. A reflection of white on a black surface. It hit Bill in the eyes, blinding him for a second. Then came the slow-motion lightning crack of a shotgun. Its Bang! Bang! replaced the lub-dub of Bill's heart. A high squeal of hot metal through air.

Ebony's eyes were round plates of fear. 'What's happening?' she screeched as they flew through the reeds.

'I don't know!' Bill answered. 'Just keep going.'

Who is shooting? thought Bill. And what, or whom, are they shooting at? Certainly not at *us*? We're just a mother and father, vacationing with kids.

Voices of warning swelled inside Bill's memory. Voices begging him to put off the family trip this year: it was no longer a safe place. They talked of terrorism and attacks. But Bill had shrugged the warnings off like beads of water: it was a *family* holiday spot; nothing bad would happen.

Reeds whipped their bellies as Bill and Ebony shot forward. Panic laced their veins as another bullet scarred the sky, closer than before. Ebony ducked and let out a squawk of fright.

Bill heard a rustling ahead. Movement. He froze. Ebony didn't.

A man, a foreigner, rose up from the long grass. Dressed in camouflage, a face striped with black paint, and two ammunition belts forming a bold X across his chest.

He levelled the sights of his rifle right at them. 'What do we have here?' he whispered. 'Two blackies!'

The barrel was two deep, unblinking eyes, and Bill stared right into them.

'Ebony, get down!' Bill ducked behind a patch of scrub as a loud crack sliced the morning in two: Bill on one side and Ebony on the other.

She screamed and faltered and fell and did not get up.

In that instant, Bill's heart stopped beating. For what is a heart without the love of its other half?

The killer crept forward and checked for a sign of life in Ebony's limp body. Finding none, the man stood, his eyes narrowed, flicking back and forward across the still grass in which Bill remained huddled. The only movement: his expanding and shrinking chest as he silently gasped and gasped for breath. Seconds passed. The world continued turning. And the man picked Ebony up as if she weighed nothing at all, as if she had never been full of the greatest amount of love, or life. With her body now flopped with emptiness, Ebony was carried away.

If Bill had been able to think of his children – had been able to think of anything at all apart from his murdered wife – he may not have left his hiding spot and followed the man.

Ebony can't be dead. She just can't be; it's a mistake. This isn't happening to me. I have a wonderful life, a beautiful family, and I've just been promoted to Head Flyer in my piloting company. I'm just an ordinary Joe.

He could call for help, but that would not bring Ebony back.

He could go after her murderer and exact revenge, but that would not bring Ebony back.

He could shrivel up into a ball of tears, but that would not bring Ebony back.

There was only one way in which he could reunite with the beating of his heart.

With his head weighed low by grief, his chin touching his chest, Bill followed in the footsteps of the assassin who had taken his wife away – and who was now the only one with the power to give her back.

The gunman turned at the sound of Bill's voice; no words, just pure pain. His cracked lips formed an O. Then he blinked, smiled, whispered, 'Hey there, blackie,' and raised his shotgun once more.

The blast erupted from the gun and shot down all the lingering colours from the sky. Blackness enveloped. In that eternal instant, two lovers met again in a sunrise that existed on the other side of mortality.

*

The sun lowered itself into the cool water, quenching its fire of day. All was quiet now, a perfect silence to welcome the coming darkness. Tiny waves rippled out to the edges of the lake as three hungry and frightened Pacific Black ducklings paddled on the surface, searching in vain for their parents, who had failed to return to the nest.

one more glass

The cork screeched as it was pulled from the bottle's neck. It gripped feebly at the smooth sides of the glass, trying to remain in its comfortable home, but all attempts were fruitless. If anything, it further irritated the man who desperately tried to get at the sweet wine, which the cork held trapped beneath.

Plucked from the bottle to a freedom it did not want, the cork was flung through the air, crashing against the wall of the man's lounge room. It dropped with a quiet thud behind the television set, atop a large pile of previously discarded and forgotten wine corks.

Judging from the amount of rubbish and dust-bunnies that formed this tiny mountain, the cork knew that sadly it would remain here for some time.

Perhaps for all time.

*

The darkness was gone. Finally gone. With a screech and

pop, the cork was removed and brilliant, pure light flowed into the wine's world. It mixed through the cool red liquid, and the wine breathed a long-awaited sigh of contentment.

The bottle tipped, and wine sloshed forward, eager to escape its glass prison. As it pooled into a large goblet, it swirled and sloshed up the sides of this new container, exploring, and reveling in the freedom it had found at last. It caught the light and refracted it around the room in a multitude of dazzling reds.

However, this feeling of liberation did not last long; the wine realized it could not exist without containment. It could never be free.

Be it bottle, goblet, or stomach, the wine knew that sadly it would remain imprisoned for some time.

Perhaps for all time.

*

Luis poured the wine into his large goblet. Anticipation surged through his body, as it always did after a night of sleep-forced sobriety. With a sigh, he plopped himself down on his tattered couch and lifted the full goblet to his pursed lips. His hands shook. Precious drops spilled over the edge of the glass and fell to freedom, joining other red wine stains on his unwashed jeans and carpet.

Fruity liquid – a wet promise of escape from this world – soaked into Luis's tongue, and he relaxed. His hands stopped shaking and he raised the glass high, a salute of gratitude, to the large painting on the wall. In bold oil, a handsome young man reclined. Long brown hair flowed over his naked shoulder; one arm pillowed his head, while the other held a glass of burgundy liquid. The crown of vine leaves adorning his head was the only thing he wore. That, and an inviting, mysterious smile. He was Dionysus: Greek God of wine and frenzy. Of theatre and illusion. And also, of Luis.

'Morning Mr. D,' Luis said to the painting, then took a second long swallow of the wine, draining the glass. He smiled and closed his eyes, concentrating on feeling the wine as it moved through his body. It filled his empty stomach, seeped through the walls into his bloodstream then up into his brain. Slowly, that all-encompassing numbness began to take over both body and mind. Most people considered this to be drunkenness, intoxication, inebriation. But Luis knew the truth; it was the blessed feeling of being filled with the Holy Spirit. The power of Dionysus was inside him; for Dionysus was not only the God of wine, he was the wine itself.

Luis knew he shouldn't drink so much. His liver was shot. His kidneys not much better. His balance gone. And whenever he could trickle out a small stream of urine, it was red; sometimes no amount of straining over the toilet bowl could bring on any bladder relief at all. The doctor had warned him that he was standing on Death's door, and if he didn't quit drinking, he would definitely be invited over that threshold. And then there was Luis's family; they used to be on his back about it all the time. They never quit nagging. They said they had his best interests at heart, but what did they know about his best interests? That's why he'd moved away and hadn't spoken to any of them in over three years.

So yes, he was sick, but he was happy. He had Dionysus to look out for him, he had his bottles of cheap red wine stacked over in the corner, and therefore, he had his freedom.

By early afternoon, Luis was into his third bottle, and deeply ensconced in a one-sided conversation with the portrait on the wall when Dionysus blinked and sat up from his laid-back position. His smile widened.

Luis dropped his glass and the spilled wine soaked into the thirsty carpet.

'Do not be afraid, Luis,' said Dionysus, 'for you are my follower, and therefore I pose no threat to you. Please, refill your glass and drink with me.' The God's voice was deep, resonant. Its soothing timbre produced the same effect over Luis as did a first mouthful of wine.

'I have been with you for many years, Luis. Guiding you. Watching as you drank my wine and followed my way. You have proved yourself worthy. Now I offer you a proposition.'

Luis swallowed, his mouth dry. With his hands shaking again, he refilled his glass and gulped down its contents.

'Luis,' Dionysus continued, his eyes burned like a fire made of secrets. 'Will you come with me?'

'Where to?' Luis whispered.

'To a place of enchantment where all your dreams will be fulfilled. You have served me well for so many years, I feel you deserve to know what it has all been for.' Dionysus raised one eyebrow. 'Don't you?'

'Yes,' Luis stuttered. 'What must I do?'

'Simply drink one more glass.'

'And then what?'

'Then you will be free.'

'Free of what?'

'Free to accompany me.'

Pondering this for a second – only a second though, for the temptation was too great – Luis topped up his glass and put it to his lips. His hands shook worse than ever now, but alcohol withdrawal was no longer the cause: fear had gripped him in its cold grasp. Fear of what though, Luis did not know; he had no reason to fear Dionysus.

The sweet liquid trickled down Luis's throat; the coldness welled and sloshed in his belly. Luis closed his eyes, sighing deeply, releasing all air from his lungs.

'Luis?'

'Yes?'

'Open your eyes.'

Luis did as he was told. Then sucked in a breath at the sight before him. Dionysus was no longer just an animated painting; the God towered before Luis, as tall as the ceiling. His features now different. His eyes, his smile... something changed.

Dionysus held out a large hand. 'Come.'

'Wait,' said Luis. 'Maybe this wasn't such a good idea. I don't think I want to go with you after all.'

Dionysus smiled. 'It's too late to change your mind.'

'Why?'

Dionysus pointed to the couch.

When Luis turned, he saw himself slumped, his eyes closed, his hand slackened and no longer gripping the glass that had fallen to the floor. His chest was not moving; no breath entered or exited his body.

'I'm... I'm *dead?*'

'Yes, Luis. That was your choice.'

'No it wasn't! You said you would show me what my service to you has all been for. You said nothing about death!'

'You chose to take my path, and now you must come with me.'

'I will not!' Luis felt his lip tremble, and bit down on it. 'You can enable resurrection: make me live again; I'm not ready to die. I realize now that I have wasted my life. Please, I beg of you, grant me one more chance to make everything right.'

'And what will you do with your life if I grant you this last chance?'

'I'll start looking after myself, I'll make amends with my family, I'll quit drinking...'

'Traitor!' Dionysus roared. The vine leaves that crowned his head started to grow with such a speed that Luis had trouble following them. They weaved and twisted down the glistening body of Dionysus. Crossed the floor. Writhed up Luis's ankles. Legs. Hips. Chest. Shoulders. Neck.

With his arms pinned to his sides and his eyes the only thing not covered by vine leaves, Luis stood and watched the furious God tremble over him.

'How dare you renounce me, Luis! After everything I have done for you. I have given you years of divine ecstasy, offered you an eternity of continued Dionysiac freedom, and you repay me by seeking sobriety? Fool!'

Luis now understood the changes he'd perceived in the face of Dionysus; his godly countenance had not altered, Luis was just able to see the truth. In death, he recognised what he had failed to see in life. The eyes of Dionysus were not merely mysterious; they were dangerous. The smile had not been inviting him; it had been entrapping him. Although this God was only a character in stories of ancient Greek mythology, he was no myth. He was real. *Is* real. Always there, making everything better with just one more glass.

Dionysus yanked on the vines that wrapped Luis's phantasmic body. They cut into him. They cut through him. And he fell in pieces onto the floor. Beneath him, the wine stains became metaphoric blood from the life he had slowly murdered.

Piece by piece, Dionysus gathered Luis in his great hands, then stepped back into the painting. Luis knew that sadly he would remain there for some time.

Perhaps for all time.

*

On the wall of the messy lounge room, the painting hung, surveyed, voyeured. The self-portrait of the artist, posing as the Greek God of wine, looked on sadly as the man on the couch spoke to him in a slurring drunken drawl, took one last gulp of his drink, then closed his eyes on life.

For years, the painting had watched this man build up a wall of solitude and distance.

How long, wondered the painting, would the man's empty, stinking body remain undiscovered? And how long would the painting be forced to hang on this wall, in this lounge room, in this house, guarding the corpse of this alcoholic?

The painting used to hang on the wall of a clean and bright exhibition building, opposite a large window that looked out at total freedom. But then the man had walked by, and the painting had been removed and brought to this place, where it was never bright, and certainly never clean. For years, it had dreamed of being removed and hung on a wall that once again overlooked freedom.

But the painting knew that sadly it would remain here for some time.

Perhaps for all time.

the other side of the mirror

Old food wrappers, used theatre tickets, discarded drink bottles, and scrunched cigarette packets all waltz with the wind along the dirty street. Invisible partners-of-air spin and dip the litter around the feet of a man who watches their performance with a solemnness that drags his face downwards.

Even the rubbish has someone to dance with, he thinks.

As he walks away, his eye is caught and held by a colorful poster beside the door to an old theatre. Moving forward for a closer look, his wearied reflection mirrors in the glass, replacing that of the handsome young actor in the playbill. Above his face, in big letters, is the play's title: *The Other Side of the Mirror*, and underneath it, a caption reads: *Take a trip to the other side 12pm weekdays.*

Plastered over this is a bright orange sticker: *Final show today!*

Why would there be a current production here? He frowns at the rotten, wooden boards nailed over the windows, and then back at the crisp, new poster behind its dirty glass frame.

Intrigued, the man looks at his watch: 11:55am.

Why not? He shrugs through the stiff-hinged theatre doors into the lobby.

Cobwebs and dust glow in the threads of light streaming through the boarded-up windows. In the center of the room, a ticket booth – as empty as the foyer surrounding it – waits for him like a lonely island.

The man calls out a polite hello, but there is no reply. On the booth wall hangs a faded 1957 calendar, and on the counter beside a tarnished silver bell sits a cardboard sign, yellowed with age and so covered in dust the words are unreadable. He wipes at the grimy sign and flowingly-penned words appear beneath his fingertips: *Please ring bell for service.*

The sweet ringing echoes through the lobby, calling out for assistance, but still no one answers.

'Hello?' the man calls again. He waits. Draws a sad face in the thick dust on the counter. 'Is anyone here? Hello!'

When silence is again the only one to greet him, he shakes his head at his own stupidity and turns to step toward the door.

'I'm sorry about the wait, Mister. How may I help you?'

This sudden voice from behind makes the man jump. He spins back around.

Dressed in a red bow tie and a white shirt, a handsome young man smiles from inside the ticket booth.

'How did you do that?' asks the man.

'Do what?'

'Get in there so fast? I only turned my back for a second.'

The ticket-seller just smiles. 'What can I do for you?'

'One ticket for the noon show, please.'

'Excellent!'

The man pulls his falling-to-pieces wallet from his back pocket. 'How much?'

The ticket-seller slides a ticket over the filthy counter top. 'It's on me; just don't tell the boss.'

'Oh! Thanks a lot, that's real nice of you.' Wiping the ticket on his pants, the man says, 'So, listen, what's with all the dust and cobwebs? It would have taken someone ages to get it all set up like this. Is it a theme of the play or something?'

'Something.' The ticket-seller smiles. 'Listen, Mister, you better hurry. Show's about to start. Just go through those doors over there.' He points to a set of heavy double doors at the end of the room. 'The usher will show you to your seat.'

As the man nears the mirrored doors, he sees the reflection of the ticket-seller smiling at him from the booth. Looking back to give a courtesy wave, a further thank you for the free entry, the man stops.

The booth is empty.

Puzzled, he shakes his head, turns slowly, and opens the double doors.

They swing shut behind him with a loud clap that bounces off the walls. Like the lobby, the auditorium is deserted and filthy.

The man feels a soft tap on his shoulder and he turns to see the ticket-seller standing before him. Now, however, instead of the blinding shirt and red bow tie, he is dressed in a red usher's uniform.

'Hello, Sir, and welcome to this afternoon's performance of *The Other Side of the Mirror*.'

'How did you do that?' asks the man. Goosebumps prickle his flesh.

'I'm sorry?'

'How did you beat me in here? How did you change your clothes so fast?'

The usher's forehead crinkles. 'I'm sure I don't know what you're talking about, Sir.' He holds out one gloved hand. 'May I see your ticket, please?'

'But, you've already seen my ticket!'

'No, Sir, I don't believe I have.'

The man hands his ticket over. 'But, I just got it from you. Out in the lobby?'

The usher smiles and tears the ticket down the middle. Handing the stub back, he says, 'No Sir, wasn't me. This way.' He spins around and walks down the aisle, all the way to the first row. Pointing with his flashlight, he says, 'That's you, there. Front row, center: best seat in the house!'

'Uh, thanks.' Confusion swirls like smoke inside the man's brain, making everything around him look foggy and unclear.

'Enjoy the show.' And the usher disappears as quickly as his fading words.

The man wipes the sticky webs off his chair, then bangs on the cushion. Dust puffs around him and forces its way in through his mouth, nostrils, eyeballs. He coughs and sits down.

They could at least turn the heat on, he thinks, hugging himself for warmth.

Looking left, then right at the empty seats, he snorts and mumbles, 'Must be one popular show!'

The lights dim and the dirty, moth-eaten curtains rise, revealing a stage that is completely empty except for a large, oval-shaped mirror. Framed in dark mahogany, the mirror sparkles in its cleanliness – a blinding contrast to the squalor that surrounds it.

When the actor steps out from behind the mirror, the man straightens in his chair.

The actor wears a wrinkled, black suit and loose tie. He has pallid and sun-starved skin. He looks hung-over and just out of bed. And yet, this stubbled, disheveled actor is the very same rosy-cheeked and healthy looking person who had sold the man his ticket, and then shown him to his seat.

'What the hell...?'

The actor comes around to face his reflection in the mirror. His shoulders droop, his arms hang, and his right hand grips a pistol with white-knuckled fingers.

For a time there is silence. The actor is nothing but a human statue on stage, staring at himself. Seconds pass. Minutes. Still nothing. The man shifts in his seat.

Then: 'Opening monologue...'

Although the first words out of the actor's mouth are barely above a whisper, the man jumps, his heart hammers his ribs, squeezes his lungs.

'...Opening monologue. Every night it's the same thing. I'm sick to death of this damn opening monologue. Sick to death of this damn play. Sick to death of everything. Sick to death of me. Look at me! How did I get here? How did I become this shadow of a human being? I used to have a wonderful life. I had great friends, a beautiful wife, an amazing home, a loving dog... I had it all. Until one of my great friends slept with my beautiful wife, who kicked me out of my amazing home, took my loving dog, and completely wrecked my wonderful life.

'You!' The actor points at the man, who jumps in his seat again. 'You know what I'm talking about, right?'

The man looks around at the non-existent people sitting either side of him.

'Yes, I'm talking to you.' The actor takes a step forward. 'I *have* to be talking to you, don't I? There's no one else in here!' He nods. 'Yeah, you know exactly what I'm going through; you've been there before.'

The man's shy smile shrinks.

'You don't need to answer me,' says the actor. 'I can see it in your eyes. They're so familiar it's like I'm looking at myself in a mirror: the sadness, the emptiness, the goddamn loneliness.' He closes his eyes and whispers, 'Drives you mad, doesn't it?'

The man stares in empty silence. Entranced.

'Like, the other day,' the actor continues, 'I was walking down the street and there was this leaf being blown around by the wind, and I thought to myself: everyone has a partner except me. Even that leaf has a partner! I was jealous of a goddamn *leaf* and a gust of *wind!*' The actor laughs, a single high-pitched cackle, before his voice fades to a rough whisper again. 'You ever feel like that?'

Still the man says nothing, driven mute by fear, confusion, and coincidence.

At the front of the stage, the actor squats, bouncing on his heels to find his balance. 'She kicked you out, didn't she? Ran off with someone else?'

The man's eyes widen and he nods slowly, breaking the spell that held him. 'How did you know about that?'

'I told you,' says the actor. 'It's your eyes. I've been seeing the same eyes in the mirror for too long. I can recognize brokenness. What was her name?'

'Her name?'

'Yeah.' The actor snarls, 'What was the bitch's name?'

'I'd rather not–'

'Sophie?'

The man draws a breath. 'How did you...? Wait, I know what this is.' He smiles again. 'You've set all this up, haven't you?' He laughs. 'Yeah, I get it now; it's all part of the show, isn't it? You do a little bit of research, and then...' He trails off. And then *what*? he thinks. Confusion fogs up his mind again. '...And then somehow get me to come and see the show... Wait a minute, how...?'

The actor continues on as if the man had not said a word. 'Did you ever think about ending it all?'

'Excuse me?'

'When she left you, did you ever consider it?'

'Consider what?'

'Come on, you know what I'm talking about.' The actor lifts the gun and presses it to his temple. 'BANG!'

The man squirms in his seat. 'That's a little personal.'

'You *did* consider it; I can see that in your eyes, too. You see,' he sits down on the edge of the stage with his long legs dangling over, 'there's that certain glimmer of hopelessness visible in your eyes, hidden behind everything else. Only people who have the same glimmer inside them can recognize it in someone else.'

'I don't know how, or why, you're doing this to me, but...'

'But you couldn't do it, could you? Didn't have the balls.'

'Are you a psychic? Is that it? You are, aren't you! And you've incorporated it into a play?' The man nods. 'Clever?'

'Let me ask you something.' The actor cocks his head to the side. 'Are you a religious man?'

'If you're psychic, you already know the answer to that.'

The actor smiles. 'Let's say you *are* a religious man; therefore you know what the sin is for killing yourself?'

The man shrugs. 'Sure, everyone knows that; you go to Hell.'

'Exactly! Eternal damnation. Now, that ain't too appealing to someone like me, and it probably wasn't too appealing to you either, which is why you are still here – lucky for me. So, you must be able to understand my dilemma: I don't particularly want to burn in Hell for all eternity, but I don't want to live in *this* Hell any longer either. I have to get out of this life... and that's where you come in.'

'Me?'

'You.'

'You mean; I get to be in the play?'

'Why don't you come up here? Come on, the stairs are just over there.'

The man looks over at the side of the stage.

'Come on; don't be shy. After all, I'm the only other person here.'

The man shrugs, stands, and joins the actor, who meets him beside the mirror. The stage lights are squintingly bright, and the man narrows his eyes as he tries to look around the empty auditorium. Then, with a knowing smile, he turns to the actor. 'See? Now I know you're a psychic. All that talk about seeing things hidden deep in my eyes; there's no way you could have seen me clearly with these bright lights blinding you!'

The actor shrugs.

'I always wanted to be an actor,' says the man, turning back to face the invisible crowd. 'Always fantasized about going back to the fifties and performing Shakespeare onstage, back when theatre was really big, you know? In one of those immaculate, ornate theatres, like this one... only a bit cleaner maybe. But, you already knew that, right?' The man moves to the front of the stage, one hand on his heart, the other reaching toward the empty seats. He clears his throat, and begins delivering his favorite line: '*All the world's a stage, and all the men and women merely—*'

'So,' the actor cuts in, 'if you wanted to be an actor so bad, why were you down there,' he points to the seat where the man had sat, '*watching* the players, instead of standing up here,' he spreads his arms wide, '*playing* the players?'

'You don't know?' asks the man.

'Enlighten me.'

'Well, I used to be a player. I was good too; everyone said I had talent. But after I got my arts degree, and Sophie and I got married, we decided that I should find a real job.'

'*Who* decided?'

The man takes a deep breath. 'She did.' He looks down at his fumbling hands. 'I gave up my dream of being an actor to work a nine to five job making fertilizer. It paid well, and Sophie was happy, so I couldn't really complain. And I still performed; whenever Sophie was out of the house, I read lines in front of the bedroom mirror. I didn't want her to know; she thought acting was a waste of time. I guess that's one good thing about being on my own so much now: I can perform as much as I like.' He turns to look into the mirror, and the smile that graces his old lips, fades. 'I gave up on myself. I failed.'

The actor's face reddens. 'At least you can live with the thought that you *might* have made it! The thought that maybe you aren't a loser like me! A talentless hack! Don't talk to me about failure. I tried – I didn't give up on myself, and I failed anyway. I've got my own play here; been running it for two solid weeks now, and you're the *first* person I've had in the audience! They're closing me down. This is my last show.'

'I'm really sorry,' says the man, meeting the actor's angry gaze in the reflection of the mirror. 'If it's any consolation, I think the play is great so far.'

'Well,' says the actor, taking a calming breath, 'you should be grateful that you're here for my finale. Not that there would even *be* a finale without you! I'll show them; you just wait. I'm going out with a bang! Which, incidentally, is where you come into it... on *bang*.' He holds out the pistol, aiming it at the man's back.

The man's face pales and he raises two shaking hands above his head. 'Please, don't...'

'What's the matter?' says the actor. 'I thought you wanted to die?'

'Not like this!'

'I could end it all for you. Right now. One click and it's over. What do you say?'

As he turns from the mirror to face the actor, the man tries to swallow his fear but it sticks in his throat. He looks from the gun, to the actor, to the gun again, unsure of which he is most frightened.

The actor's face contorts into a grin; he starts to laugh. 'Sorry, I couldn't resist. I'm just playing with you, man.' He wipes a tear from his left eye, then flips the gun, handle out, toward the man. 'Take it.'

The man lets out his held breath, and lowers his hands. 'That wasn't funny. You scared the Hell out of me!'

'I'm sorry.' The actor tries to keep his face serious,

but a laugh escapes through his nose and he snorts loudly.

'No, it's okay.' A thin smile turns up the corners of the man's lips. 'I should have known you weren't serious. As if this gun is really loaded!' He takes the gun from the actor and studies it. 'So, do I have any lines? What do you want me to do?'

The actor's smile vanishes. 'I want you to kill me. I can't do it myself – eternal damnation and all that, remember? But, if I am *murdered*... well... that's not my fault, is it?'

'No... I guess not.'

'See? It makes perfect sense! So? Will you do it? Will you shoot me?'

'Of course! I finally get to be in a play, a *real* play, with a very important role. It might not be Shakespeare, but it *is* a tragedy of sorts. I'm not going to turn that down; what do you think I am, crazy?'

'Great!' The actor claps the man on the shoulder. 'You're sure doing me a favor, buddy. I won't forget this when I'm standing in front of the Big Guy. I'll be sure to put in a good word for you.'

'So, you want me to just shoot you here, right in the middle of the stage?'

The actor nods once. 'That's the plan. And don't worry about the police or anything. You wont be arrested for murder; I've written you a note.' He takes a folded piece of paper from his breast pocket, and hands it to the man.

'What's this?'

'Read it.'

The man unfolds the letter and begins to read.

'Out loud.' The actor rolls his eyes.

'Oh, sorry. *There is no one left on this earth who cares enough about me to be upset over my death; no one to whom I wish to apologize over my leaving, or to farewell. Therefore I bequeath all my worldly possessions to this one friend...*' The man pauses and looks at the actor. 'Me?'

'You.'

'Thanks.'

The actor smiles and nods. 'Just repaying the favor.'

Looking down at the neat handwriting once again, the man continues: '*... this one friend who has helped me find the freedom I've been looking for. This person is not to be held responsible for my death in any way. If anything, he should be praised. He is the one person who actually cared! Perhaps in death, I will achieve the fame I sought in life.*'

Pointing to the letter, the man asks, 'Is this really your signature here on the bottom?'

'Of course; I wouldn't forge my name on a suicide note!'

'You think I could keep this? I mean; I know you probably need it for your next show and all, but I'd really like it, you know, as a souvenir?'

'*Next* show?' The actor's forehead creases. 'I told you

before: this is my last performance – if you can even call it that. But yeah, it's yours. *All* my belongings will go to you once I'm dead; that letter included.'

The man shakes his head. 'You don't break character for a second, do you? Amazing.'

'Can't you see the genius of all this?' A smile turns to a wide grin on the actor's face. 'No one has ever written their actual murder into a play before. No one has ever written their death into a play, and performed it on a stage! It's the ultimate form of Method Acting; Lee Strasburg would be so proud! And so what if there are no other people here to witness it? It'll still go down in history as one of the greatest acting sacrifices of all time. Don't you think?'

The man opens his mouth to answer, but the actor keeps on talking.

'It's brilliant! Two birds with one bullet: I'll be dead, and we'll both be famous actors! Then you can really stick it to that bitch, Sophie.'

'Now *that* sounds good to me. So when do I do this? Do I wait a bit longer, say some lines, and pull the trigger at the end of the play so you...' his fingers form quotation marks, '...*die* just before the curtains come down? Make it a big finale? Or do I just do it now?'

The actor takes a deep breath and steps toward the man until the barrel of the gun presses against his stomach. He takes the note back and clenches it in his left fist. 'I'm ready whenever you are, my friend.' His voice is a whisper.

The man leans forward, as if there are others around them who might overhear his next words. 'I have to say; before I do this, this whole including-an-audience-member-in-the-show-thing: it's a great idea. This is all so exciting!'

'You do understand that this is not my normal show, don't you?' asks the actor. 'You really are about to kill me?'

'Yeah, yeah, okay sure,' says the man, then leans forward again. 'Listen, what happens after I shoot you? I mean, the play isn't even half over yet, is it? No, no don't tell me; let it be a surprise.'

'Listen, man, I already told you; this isn't...' but the actor stops, and after a second of thought, reconsiders his words. 'Actually, you're absolutely right. It *would* wreck it if I told you what happens next. You'll just have to wait and see.'

'Okay, are you ready?' asks the man, a childish grin lights up his face.

'Yes,' says the actor. 'Shoot.' He closes his eyes and holds his breath. Sweat beads on his upper lip and temples.

The man pulls the trigger.

The gun booms.

The sound echoes around the auditorium, smashing

violently into the man as it ricochets back at him from the walls. He stumbles.

The actor gasps and staggers backward, clutching his middle.

'Jesus Christ! The gun was *loaded*!' The man throws the pistol. 'I'm sorry, I'm so sorry, I didn't know! I'll get help!'

As the man reaches the stage steps, the actor calls out: 'No, wait! You already *have* helped me.' He straightens up.

No bullet pierces his stomach. No blood darkens his shirt. He smiles.

'Oh, thank God! You really had me for a second there.' The man's laughter is flooded with relief. 'I thought I had shot you for real!'

'I'm sorry for tricking you,' says the actor, closing the distance between them, 'but it was the only way. You would never have had the strength to go through with it otherwise.'

'Go through with what?'

The actor presses his lips into a pitying smile and looks down at the man's stomach.

Blood flows from a wound in the man's gut. He touches it and his hand comes away red. His breathing becomes rapid; he starts to whimper in agony, in fright, in confusion. Pain sweeps his feet from under him and he collapses to his knees.

'What's going on? Who shot me?' The man doubles over, gripping his bleeding stomach.

The actor crouches down beside the man and meets his tear-filled eyes in the reflection of the mirror. '*You* did. No eternal damnation for you. All the world's a stage, remember, my friend? We are merely the players. Our scripts have already been written. Yours. Mine. Even the people out there who watch us perform them. We have no control over our shows; if it is written, then so it shall be.' He places a hand on the man's back. 'I'm sorry. I had no control over this. *You* had already written it.'

'Who are you?' The man whispers.

The room spins. He squeezes his eyes shut as the floor catches him.

When he opens his eyes, the auditorium is gone. The stage has vanished. The theatre no longer exists. He is curled before the mirror in his own dirty, dusty and cobweb-filled bedroom. Alone.

A pistol lies beside him on the floor.

Clenched in his left hand is a suicide note.

And beside him is a hand-written script entitled *The Other Side of the Mirror.*

the saving grace

'Jesus.' Hamish stopped his van at the gates, but it was neither the blinding gleam of 14-karat gold, nor the intricate metalwork spelling *EDEN* in three-foot-high letters that dropped his jaw and widened his eyes. 'Whoa.'

Along the driveway, out into the street, and around the corner, people lay on the ground. Some had tents, some had sleeping bags, some only had each other. Empty pizza boxes, milk cartons and dirty nappies littered the sidewalk. Even with the window shut tight, the stench of unwashed bodies and dried fecal matter seeped into Hamish's car.

It must be rank out there, he thought. And as the window rolled down and he leaned out to state his name and business into the speaker, he gagged on the sour air that slapped his face like an open hand.

'Christ,' he muttered, breathing through his mouth. 'My name is Hamish, I'm with S.A.F.E. Home Security.'

'Are there any other persons in your vehicle, Sir?' asked the voice from the intercom.

'Just me.'

'Very good,' came the reply. 'Please drive through the gates. The butler will meet you at the house.'

Hamish inched his car forward just as a woman with a patch over one eye ran up and leaned in his window. 'Wait!' Her breath was worse than the fecal matter. 'You going in?' She grabbed his arm. 'Here...' Pulling off a diamond ring, she held it out. 'Give *me* your appointment! I'm going blind, and I just want to see my granddaughter – she'll be born in the new year, and I just want to see her little face once. Please!'

'Blind?' laughed a man, whose nose was a puss-filled concavity in his face. 'At least you'll still be around.' He pushed the lady away, and she stumbled and fell, as he stuffed fistfuls of cash into Hamish's lap. 'Look at me! This disease is eating my face. Pretty soon all the flesh will be gone from my jaw and I wont be able to eat! I'm going to starve! Please, let *me* go in your place?'

Then a third man approached the car. And a fourth. Someone tapped a cane on the passenger window and two more people scrambled onto the roof.

'Hey!' Hamish yelled at them, and inched the car forward again. 'I'm only here to upgrade the security!'

'Do you even realize where you are?' said the man without a nose.

Hamish shrugged at him.

'This is Eve Eden's house!'

'*The* Eve Eden?'

The man nodded.

Now it all made sense. All these people were just like him. Willing to give anything, to do anything, for one chance at The Cure.

'It don't happen often, but when there's a cancelation Eve will see the first in line. And sometimes, people with an appointment will sell it for the right price. Don't happen often though; last I heard, the waiting list for an appointment was three years! Probably even longer by now.'

'That's crazy,' said Hamish.

'Specially since most of us don't have three years to wait.'

Hamish shook his head and thought of his own ticking clock. 'Three years is far too long.'

A green light flashed above the intercom.

'I'm really sorry,' said Hamish, handing back the man's money. 'I wish there was something I could do.'

The man without a nose stepped back, and the rest of the people scurried away.

The bars of the gate were made of the latest gold-light, and Hamish's van sliced through the holographic structure. There was a buzzing as the beams scanned the car, searching for any other bodies besides Hamish's.

In the rearview mirror, the man without a nose raised

his hand in a small wave before shrinking to nothing with distance.

I'm in the Garden of Eden, Hamish thought to himself as he drove around the winding path. Holy shit. Grace will not believe this! The Garden of God Damned Eden! Would my prayers be heard in here? Surely, this would be the one place where prayers amplified?

But God wasn't listening. Not even here in the Garden of Friggen Eden, not with the thousand others lined up outside, each one clasping their hands around a seed of hope just as precious as his own.

Maybe God had granted more prayers a hundred years ago. Back when the only proof of God was blind faith. Back when some actually *laughed* at the thought of prayer!

Back before the second coming.

When Jesus Christ had returned in 2014, he brought with Him incontrovertible scientific proof of a higher being: the actual DNA of God. He then disappeared again, although sightings became common; every few years He would be seen working in a drive-through, or riding the number seven bus with His head in a book. He'd perform some little miracle, and would then vanish once more.

When scientists got hold of His DNA, they cloned it, and injected it into humans, creating a cure for every disease and ailment in existence. Everything from a common cold to cancer healed instantly. But after years with no sickness-related deaths, an overpopulation of bodies on this already crowded planet had forced the government to restrict The Cure to those of the highest-income bracket.

The rich and powerful could now buy near immortality, while the rest of the population withered and died out.

As each generation of the rich continued to thrive, the price of The Cure rose, slowly culling even those who had previously been able to afford it.

'You must be Hamish?' A man sitting on the front steps of the grand house unfolded himself. He had shoulder length hair, a scruffy blonde beard, an open necked shirt, and bare feet.

'Yes,' said Hamish. 'I'm supposed to wait for the butler.'

'That's me.' He grinned. 'The name's Xavier!'

'*You* are a butler?'

'I don't much care for penguin suits and white gloves. And watch out if anyone comes at me with scissors!' He brushed a hand through his hair. 'I see you made it through the huddled mass at the gate.' Xavier frowned sadly toward the driveway.

'Yeah.' Hamish shook his head. 'Can't blame them, though; we'll give anything for The Cure.'

'*We?*' asked Xavier.

Hamish pressed his lips into a hard line, trying to keep the words locked away. He didn't like saying them out loud; it made things too real. But what if this guy could get a message to Eve for him? Hamish took a breath. 'One year,' he said. 'One damned year and my son, Bodhi, will be dead. My little boy won't live to see the year twenty-one fifteen.'

'You don't qualify for The Cure, then?' asked Xavier.

Hamish coughed a laugh. 'Who does anymore?'

The butler nodded, sadly. 'Yes, it should never have come to this.'

'Why should *they* get to live, and we have to suffer and die? Or worse,' Hamish said, 'watch the ones we love suffer and die.'

'Yeah, life's a tough bag,' said Xavier. 'And I'm sorry to hear about your boy. Sucks. A father should never have to see his child go.'

'Thank you.'

Xavier shook the hair out of his face. 'Come on, I'll show you what we need upgraded.'

Hamish grabbed his equipment and followed the butler down a stone path, through a garden – through *the* garden – and stopped at the foot of a massive apple tree.

'Is that...?' Hamish stared up into the overhanging branches.

Xavier nodded. 'That's the tree. It's got a standard three point three series light wall around it, but Eve wants it upgraded to a seven point nine. Every now and then someone breaks through and strips it bare. Do you know how much forbidden fruit goes for on the black market these days!'

But Hamish just stared up through the swaying branches above.

Laughing softly, Xavier handed Hamish written instructions, patted him on the back, and then left him alone with the tree and his own awe.

Hamish gaped in the cold shadows of the most famous tree in all of history. The Tree of Knowledge of Good and Evil. And there were the apples, the famous apples, gleaming red, and perfectly round. Holy shit! Just wait until he told Grace about this! He'd thought it was shocking enough to be inside the grounds of the Garden of Eden, but to stand among the roots of the actual tree itself? Shit. Grace was going to die!

The snap of a stem echoed through Hamish's bones and he jumped, startled, as an apple fell to the grass with a cushioned thunk as soft as pure hope. He bent slowly to his knees and with two hands enclosed his fingers over the cool hard skin of the fruit.

What if I just slipped it into my bag and took it home to feed to Bodhi? Could The Cure be that simple to obtain?

His fingers began to shake as he opened the latch of his satchel.

'It doesn't work that way.'

Hamish dropped the apple and spun around. 'I'm sorry!' His heart pounded as he gazed up into the beautiful face of Eve Eden, the First Woman, the one from whom we all descended.

Throughout all of time, She and Adam had been guardians of this tree. As punishment for tasting the forbidden fruit, they were forced to live an immortal existence – to watch their family die off, at first one by one, and then thousands by thousands as the human population grew.

Eve nodded to the shiny red apple on the grass. 'The miracle is not in the fruit. It is in the giver.' She stooped with a liquid gracefulness and lifted the apple from the grass to her mouth, sinking in her teeth with a sharp crack of piercing skin, and leaving a glossy shine of juice on her lips. 'This apple…' she smiled, swallowing, '…is just an apple. And had you slipped it into your satchel you would have taken nothing with you but a stolen piece of fruit.'

'I wasn't going to…'

'It's all right.' She waved a hand through the air. 'It's *Hamish*, isn't it?'

He nodded.

'For whom did you want this apple, Hamish?'

'My son has cancer.'

'Ah.' She nodded. 'Cancer. I get that one a lot.'

'He is only five! I'll do anything.' Hamish's voice cracked. 'I'll do absolutely *anything* to save my boy.'

Eve nodded. 'I can cure your boy.'

'Oh.' Hamish's hand came up to cover his mouth.

'But,' she held up a finger, 'for his life, I would need another of equal merit in it's place.'

'What?' he whispered.

'You said you'd do anything?'

He pressed his lips. 'All right. If my son will live, I am prepared to give my life for his.'

Eve smiled, and then began to laugh softly. 'No, it's not *your* life that is equal to your son's.'

'Then who...'

'Your *wife's*.' Eve took a second bite of the apple and the crack of pierced skin slapped into Hamish like an open palm against his cheek.

'You want me to kill... my wife?'

'No.' She shook her head and licked the juice from her lips. 'I want you to *save your son*.'

Raising her hand into the branches of the tree, Eve pulled down a second apple and held it out to Hamish. He took a step backwards as if the fruit was about to explode and destroy his entire world.

'What...' He cleared his throat. 'What will happen...?'

'She must not know,' said Eve. 'When she takes a bite, a piece of apple will lodge in her throat, blocking off her airway and suffocating her.'

'Christ.' Hamish took another step away.

'It will not be quick. It will not be painless. And you will witness the entire thing.'

'I can't.'

'If you complete this task,' said Eve, 'come back and

see me. And I will make sure your son will be healthy again.'

'But I love my wife!'

'The question is not whether you love your wife; the question is whether you love your wife *more* than your child.' She stepped forward and this time Hamish did not back away. 'The choice is yours.'

*

Hamish stood in his kitchen staring into the open satchel. Inside, the apple shone with both the beauty of gain, and the horror of sacrifice.

'I didn't hear you come in, Hamish.'

Hamish closed the bag in one quick movement and turned to face his wife. Her skin was smooth and pale, her eyes a piercing green, her hair a wavy auburn-gold – the exact shade their son inherited. She was still the most beautiful woman he had ever seen; a fact that startled him after every absence.

'Oh, Grace!' Wrapping his arms around her, he pressed his face into her neck and breathed in the scent of her skin. It was a smell like nothing else. A smell he thought he'd have for the rest of his life. But now... maybe just minutes.

'How was work?' she asked.

'Fine.'

'Anything exciting happen today?'

He didn't answer. *Couldn't* answer. What was he

supposed to say? I met Eve Eden and she gave me an apple that is going to kill you, but don't worry because at least our son will no longer have cancer!

Christ. He couldn't go through with this. He couldn't lose Grace. She was the only light he had in this dark world. The one thing that kept him sane in the wake of Bodhi's diagnosis. The only thing keeping him going was the knowledge that – no matter what happened – he would always have Grace.

But now, he had the opportunity to save his son's life. What sort of parent hesitated at this type of chance?

'What would you give,' he whispered, 'for Bodhi to be cured?'

'Hamish, please don't start this again. There's no point wishing for things we can never receive.'

'But what if there was a way...'

'I'd do *anything*.' Grace's voice hardened, gripping onto each word like it was a life preserver. 'I'd give my own *life* to save his. But let's not dwell on it. It's not going to happen. Our prayers simply are not going to be answered. We need to accept that and stop wasting time mourning a child that is still with us.'

A child that is still with us, he thought. Images of Bodhi – becoming an adult, becoming a man, becoming a father – flashed through Hamish's mind. He imagined his son cradling a son, kissing its bald head, and whispering the same words Hamish had spoken on the day of Bodhi's birth: '*I will do anything to protect you.*'

Once again, Hamish inhaled the scent of his wife's skin. 'I love you, Grace.'

'I know.' She smiled at him. 'What is with you today?'

'Nothing.' He shrugged. Then, reaching into his bag, Hamish pulled out the apple.

The overhead lights in the kitchen bounced off its shiny skin in spiky shards.

'Grace,' he whispered. 'This is for you.'

*

Hamish, his son in the seat beside him, once again drove up the winding driveway of Eden.

'Hamish!' Xavier unfurled on the front steps of the house and waited as Hamish and his thin, pale son approached. 'My man! What brings you back here? I thought you were done upgrading the tree?'

'I came to return this to Eve.' From his satchel, Hamish pulled out the apple. Its skin was clean and smooth and unpunctured by human teeth.

'You didn't give it to her?' Xavier grinned as he took the apple.

'I did,' said Hamish. 'But I took it back again.'

'Well done,' said Xavier. 'Well done! And this must be little Bodhi?' Xavier bounced down into a squat, eye to eye with the boy. 'Hey, little dude, how you feeling?'

'Sleepy.'

Xavier smiled and held out his palm. 'Give me five, kid.'

Bodhi slapped his hand downward and giggled as the butler moved his away at the last second.

'Too slow!' said Xavier. 'Try again.'

Bodhi's little palm smacked solidly into the wall of Xavier's hand. The clap of skin hitting skin boomed through the silent garden. Cracked and bounced off tree trunk and then tree trunk until it faded away into nonexistence.

The butler lifted his hand away and nodded. 'You take care, little dude, okay?'

'Yeah, okay,' said Bodhi. 'Daddy, can we go now?'

Hamish nodded, smiled at Xavier, and then headed back to his car.

*

'I don't believe this.' Doctor White sat opposite Hamish and Grace, and his skin was as pale as his name. 'Bodhi's cancer is completely gone!'

'How is that possible?' whispered Grace.

'I don't know,' said Dr. White. 'I honestly don't know. It's a miracle.' The doctor shook his head. 'It's almost as if the boy was touched by the healing hand of Jesus Christ, Himself.'

my mother's daughter

The computer screen is a white sheet: new, crisp, not yet slept on. Until now.

I sit and wait, not wanting to rush them, not wanting to pressure their relationship. After several minutes the magical pairing of Inspiration and Imagination begin rolling about together, gasping and groaning, wrinkling the white sheet with the ferocity of their lovemaking. And you – my precious idea – are formed and implanted like an embryo in the spongy wall of my consciousness. There, you will feed off the rich blood supply and grow into a healthy and fully-formed piece of prose.

I pause, savoring this wonderful moment of conception. My fingertips hover above the keyboard. Then with a breath I let them fall, pounding the letters. I type furiously, hurriedly, before you, my embryonic idea, come loose and bleed out of me...

*

There are clouds in the sky, heavy with the possibility of a shower, nevertheless I leave my car in the driveway and walk all the way to the mall. Everything feels different: the wind on my face, the sun's warmth on the crown of my head, the soft spring of grass under my feet. Life is heightened, all because of you.

I let my hand drift to my belly, a place to which it has been drawn ever since I discovered you in there. My stomach is still flat, and it's funny; we work to stay in shape, to stay slim, to keep a flat abdomen, embarrassed if there is the slightest bulge, but as soon as we are told that inside our trim and toned stomach a tiny person is living, we can't wait to blow up like balloons, to show off our Buddha bellies with pride. To say, hey, look what I can do: I can make people!

In the crowded shopping centre, I notice other girls my age laughing, happy, without a care in the world. So, I'm only eighteen? So what? It's just a number, right? Just because I'll soon be carrying a kid on my hip doesn't mean life will screech to a halt and the word fun will never be uttered again.

I ignore shops with platform sandals in their windows, beautiful gowns, groovy shirts, and I head straight into Baby World. I'm only ten weeks along, and you won't be here for another seven months, but why wait? And I want to make sure I'm ready.

Which color to buy? Pink or blue? I don't want to take the easy way out and go for white, or yellow, so I pick up a pink blanket with bunnies. Would you like this design? Or would you prefer the pink hearts? Or the blue teddies?

I settle on a pink rug with daisies, and a blue jumpsuit with matching sailor hat.

Half a block from home, with the first gifts I will ever buy you banging softly into my leg, I feel the slightest twinge, the beginnings of a cramp as you make tiny fists and scrabble to hold on.

That night as I lie in bed, as you bleed painfully away, I cry into your blanket until I am completely empty.

*

I read back over your words so far, my mouth squinching up like a drawstring purse. Okay, I think, you have grown from a collective mass of creative cells and have started to resemble a story. As your little heart begins to beat, a new character enters your world...

*

I don't know why I got married. I guess I loved him. We'd been together long enough. It's what people expected us to do.

After only a few months, I am rewarded with your conception and it finally dulls the loss I suffered three years ago when I had the miscarriage.

On the day I reach ten weeks, the same milestone at which I lost you last time, I lie in bed for the entire day. My pillow is wrapped in the pink baby blanket with the daisies, and I rest my head on its softness, using it to send messages of hope out to whomever may be listening.

The Husband walks in and out of the room, I don't know how many times throughout the day.

When are you getting up? When are you making breakfast? Lunch? Dinner? Why are you so depressed over something that happened three years ago? Come on, honey, get over it and focus on our future together!

Every time he leaves the room I bury my face deeper in your blanket and pray that someone can hear me.

When the cuckoo clock in the lounge strikes midnight, a wave of relief washes away the fear that has held me a prisoner in this bed.

I made it. And you are still with me.

At 12 weeks The Husband comes home from the office with a gift. A pregnancy calendar. As I read through the dates and learn about the way you are growing inside me, I discover you are two-and-a-half inches long, and you weigh 14 grams. You have the ability to swallow, and you can absorb and discharge fluids. Your face is shaped into something that resembles a human being, and inside your mouth tiny tooth buds have seeded. Your hands have perfect little fingernails. And perhaps these fingers, with their brand new calcium coverings, are waving to me as you say goodbye again.

*

I sit back, take a breath, rest my head in my hands. As you

feed off me, and your word count grows larger, you suck energy from my body like a benign growth in my brain.

*

I am only 21 when I am diagnosed with cervical cancer. They want to cut it out of me. A cone biopsy, they say; as if I'm supposed to know what that is.

There are risks, the doctor tells me. But then there are always risks with surgery.

The very small risk of never being able to will you into existence sits on one side of the scales in my mind. On the other side sit the cancerous cells that grow and mutate even as I weigh up this decision.

The next morning, The Husband drops me at the outpatient centre.

Good luck, honey, he says. I'll pick you up after it's over.

In the surgery, I strip naked and dress in a gown. A nurse helps position me on the table – on my back, feet in stirrups, in that most vulnerable of all positions for any woman.

A needle slides into my vein, an IV is taped to my skin, and anesthetic seeps its way into my blood and up into my brain. The drug walks straight up to my consciousness-lamp and wrenches out the globe.

While I am feeling my way around inside this darkness, locked inside a tiny room in my head where I feel nothing but my own thoughts, I am washed with medical soap, spread open by the speculum, and sliced by a scalpel.

When the procedure is done and the globe has been returned to my consciousness-lamp, I wait in the recovery room for almost seven hours. I wait for The Husband until it is dark outside. I wait until the nurses are looking at me with pity.

A taxi drives me home. And when I hand the driver his fare, I slip my wedding ring into his palm as well.

*

I've brewed myself a hot, sweet coffee, which banishes all sign of creative lethargy from my body. Healed, renewed, I am able to continue with your development unhindered. With my mug steaming happily beside my keyboard, I return to your story with a new vigor.

*

It is two years before I have a third chance to bring you into the world again. My life is better: there are no more abnormal cells; I have a New Man who makes me laugh and makes me think and makes me feel loved. Perhaps you knew my life was not yet perfect enough for you, and so you kept refusing to enter it until it was just right.

Just right, like the way it is now.

But maybe my world is still not perfect enough. For after 12 weeks, you leave me devastated again.

*

In the development of every story, there is a safety point, the passing of which indicates it will not be deleted and started again, or shoved in a file and forgotten about. You have now reached this stage. You will continue growing in the womb of my brain until the final full stop is in place. Nothing can stop you now.

*

At 26 years old – eight long years since I began my journey to meet you – I am told you are blooming inside me for the fourth time. In my bedroom, standing on a stool, I reach for a dust-covered shoebox. Hidden out-of-sight on top of the wardrobe, my memories can not reach me from up there to scrabble their cold hands across my heart.

After stuffing this box so full of you, I am surprised it hasn't burst open while waiting on top of the cupboard.

I sit cross-legged on the bed, the box before me, and remove the lid. I close my eyes as I open it, scared of the emotion that is about to spring out at me like a jack-in-the-box. But all that flies out is a tiny moth.

This time, I say, this time you will end up wrapped in your blanket. You've been waiting long enough! This time.

Maybe I'm superstitious, but I carry your blanket everywhere. I buy a larger handbag to stash your blanket at the bottom and no one will know. I take it to the fancy restaurant when New Man and I celebrate your existence. I take it to the sewing factory where I work every weekday. I take it to my brother's wedding. And I take it to the hospital when I learn that you have left me once again.

*

You kick me; it feels like bubbles are bursting in my mind.

It makes me smile and rub at my temples with pride that you are growing so quickly, maturing so fast. Your display of strength has proven that the vitamin of cause-and-effect I swallowed earlier has helped to maximize your potential for greatness.

*

My doctor looks up at me over the test results and clears his throat. We believe that your last miscarriage was caused by Incompetent Cervix, he says. The cone biopsy you underwent five years ago has weakened the muscles in your cervix. It will be difficult for you to carry a baby full term. I'm sorry, he says. I know this is hard for you to hear, but if you hadn't had the biopsy then the circumstances for you would be much worse. Think about it that way and maybe it will be a little easier to handle.

A little easier? I think. All I've ever wanted was to have you. Someone who would mean more than anyone else, including myself. And now I have jeopardized that. I risked your life to save my own. What kind of mother does that make me?

Maybe I don't deserve you after all?

*

You are developing nicely in your warm pouch of creative nutrients, and it is time to inject a little conflict into your bloodstream; a little bit of a shock value, a little bit of desperation, and a glimpse that your protagonist is not perfect, but flawed and quite wonderfully human...

*

When the doctor tells me I am pregnant again, I don't smile.

I cry.

I hyperventilate.

It hasn't even been a month since I lost you last time. Not even four weeks of grieving, and you have come back again.

Why? You know I am not fit to bring you into the world.

Oh, it hurts so much to lose you. The pain grows worse every time you leave. I am still raw over your previous goodbye, and there's no way I can handle another one.

Maybe it would be best, says the doctor, considering... he clears his throat. Maybe, he says, it would be best to terminate.

I nod. I agree. I drown in a sea of guilt.

I'm in the outpatient centre again. With that horrible crinkling paper gown. With my feet propped in the stirrups. With an IV in my arm. With the speculum waiting to open up the doors of my cervix and usher you out.

I'm sorry, but I'm not ready. I'm not strong enough. This time, it is I who will be saying goodbye to you.

*

You have now reached the final stretch; I am fat with your life and look forward to that exultant moment where I can click print and you will slide into the world on a cradle of crisp, white paper and slippery black ink.

*

Another two years pass and I slowly rebuild myself. I am strong again. I am ready again. And when my period is just one day late, I am at the doctor, confirming your very early existence and being admitted to the Royal Women's, where I will stay for the next forty weeks. I won't lose you this time. Not this time.

At ten weeks, I worry.

At 11 weeks, I fret.

At 12 weeks, I expect blood.

At 13, I begin to hope again.

At 15, the doctor explains a surgical procedure where my cervix will be stitched closed to prevent you slipping out. I agree, but he hesitates.

You have been making great progress, he tells me with a smile. There seems to be no indication of Incompetent Cervix. Why don't we just wait and see?

At 16 weeks, he says I can go home.

At 20 weeks – because of the doctor's incompetence as well as that of my cervix – I lose you again.

*

You are almost a fully-grown story, a fleshed-out, chubby and healthy piece of escapism. With enthusiasm, I begin to count down the lines until you are complete.

*

You have to shake off this broken heart, my friend says after my relationship with New Man collapses under the emotional strain of loss. Move on and find someone else.

And find him, I do. I meet Your Father at the party my friend drags to me to.

114

And with his help, I find you again.

Like last time, I am admitted to the Royal Woman's when I am five weeks pregnant. I refuse to leave my room, refuse to get out of bed, refuse to become vertical in case gravity reaches up and pulls you away from me.

I settle in, with my family smiling at me from photo frames around my bed, a vase full of flowers, and a few comforting knick-knacks from home, but something is missing. I need your blanket. I need it here for when you arrive.

You have to go home, I say to Your Father. Get the baby blanket.

He looks at me and raises an eyebrow. But he shrugs his shoulders, kisses my forehead, and says he'll be back soon.

I sigh and relax in the bed.

An hour later, Your Father holds out a gift bag as he waltzes back into my room. Surprise!

What's this? I ask, grinning.

Open it.

I peer over the edges of the floral cardboard bag, and then tip it upside down. A baby blanket slides out and lands in my lap.

What's this? I am not smiling anymore.

It's a racing car, what does it look like.

You bought a new blanket?

Yeah, well, I found the one you were talking about, and it was all ratty and full of holes and stains. It practically fell to pieces when I picked it up, so I threw it out and bought a new one. Do you like it?

You threw it out?

He frowns. I'm not giving my baby a dirty rag to be wrapped in.

It wasn't a rag, it was...

I stop. What am I fighting for? He's right, your blanket was just a tattered old blanket I bought 12 years ago. A new blanket is exactly what you need.

Or maybe, it's exactly what I need.

I press the soft material to my cheek. I love it, I say. Thank you.

I remain in that hospital bed, flat on my back, all day, every single day, as you grow so very slowly inside me. I use a bedpan. I have sponge baths. I get bedsores. I am bored beyond belief.

The doctors do all they can to prevent it, but I go into premature labour at 28 weeks, and after an emergency caesarean, you leave me again.

You are stolen from me and put into a humidicrib until you are strong enough to be wrapped up in your new pink baby blanket and taken home where I will love you for the rest of my life.

*

I sigh and sit back, grinning down at your pages in my hands, the ink still shining and wet.

You are born.

Don't quit before the miracle, I whisper to myself, as I always do when I give birth to a new piece of writing. It is a philosophy ingrained in my genetic makeup. It flowed through my blood as I formed. And it is the reason I *live* today.

I raise your heavy wad of pages in my arms, and imagine how you will look when you have matured, when you are sitting on a shelf alongside other printed and bound volumes. When a reader holds you in their hands and reads these very words.

Don't quit before the miracle, I say again. And I smile: I won't quit. I will never quit.

I am, after all, my mother's daughter.

dove

Chapter One

Ray

Flapping a back road of Tennessee at high noon on the last day in April 1970 I hitched the strap of Japhy's guitar higher on my aching shoulder and with my forehead scrunched mused back at the trail of footprints we'd left behind as we thumbed our way north to safety. We dragged our feet along this barren highway with no shade some miles south of the Kentucky border, and we intended to sleep beneath a friendly and protective Kentuckian oak that night and then either walk all day again or catch a ride all the way through Kentucky, Indiana, Michigan, then across the border to Toronto.

The back of Japhy's neck was sunburned red, gritty with dirt and I wanted to lean forward and press my lips against his skin. Wiping my forehead, I smiled at the image of our two shadows side by side on this earth, like two lovers stretched out on a bed.

Scratching the stubble on his cheek, Japhy turned. Diamonds of perspiration sparkled on his hairline. Sun glowed through his whiskers, tiny fires dancing on his skin. I fisted my fingers, gripping the urge to touch his cheek ever so softly. I couldn't give in; I knew where that would lead us – running for your life has a damn erotic edge to it (hell, just ask my virginity) – and we didn't have time for that right now.

'Hey, is it the thirtieth?' he asked.

I nodded.

'Today's the day, then. I'm officially a delinquent.'

I nodded again, as if that very thought hadn't been bouncing around against the inside of my skull all day hammering at my brain all day making me wince with each blow all day.

'You're doing the right thing,' I said.

He was silent. Then: 'You reckon my dad called the cops?'

'Course not.'

Japhy shrugged. 'Said he would.'

'He *won't*!'

Japhy glanced at me and raised his eyebrows.

'He was angry, that's all,' I said. 'Deep down, he's relieved you won't be going...' I paused, '...Over There.'

'You can say the word, you know.' He smiled. 'You can say *Vietnam*. It's not a jinx.'

'Don't care,' I dipped my head, and walked on. 'I'm not taking any chances.'

I would not let a mere slip of paper remove this man from my world; I would fight anybody who tried to take him away. I may not look threatening (just a girl standing five-three in heels with a flower in her hair and a peace sign around her neck) but, boy, I'll scratch out eyes if I have to.

Japhy had the kind of heart that would gladly sacrifice itself to save all the faceless people this war in Vietnam was supposedly fighting for. I, on the other hand, would gladly sacrifice all those faceless strangers – and even myself – in order to save him and his big, stupid heart. Maybe that makes me a monster? Perhaps. But it is people like Japhy that this world needs. It is people like Japhy that will one day save us all. Therefore, it is people like Japhy that need us to save them from their own stupid goodness.

I stared as Japhy's boots kicked up clouds of dust that clung to his jeans with each forward step. I stared as silver shards of light speared the dust cloud, thrown there through bullet holes in a murdered 55 Mile road sign. I stared as folk singer, James Lee Stanley, climbed aboard my brain like a little bum climbing into the car of a freight train. He winked and smiled at my look of surprise, and then sat with his back against the wall of my skull, tapped his tiny foot against my spongy brain and strummed his matchstick-sized guitar.

Japhy strode in rhythm to the beat of James's song, the rap of James's foot, the pluck of James's strings. The crunches of gravel underfoot drummed a perfect four-four melody. Crunch. Crunch. Crunch. Crunch.

Well I don't need no mighty mountain shining silver in the sun. I don't need to reach its highest peak before my days are done. I don't need the name of fame hung up on everything I do. But I need you.

Crunch. Crunch.

Oh, honey, I need you.

Crunch. Crunch.

Focusing all my attention on James's performance, I meditated on this prayer-of-sorts the musician handed me; I just grooved away, pretended that everything was cool and I wasn't worried about the FBI tracking our footsteps, or arresting Japhy, or forcing him onto the frontlines of a war with nothing to shield himself but a loaded gun. Nope, I wasn't worried about nothing. Nothing at all.

I don't know just how it happened – why I love you like I do. What you got that keeps me singing – what you got that sees me through all the bad times and the good times, baby, the times between the two. I need you.

Bouncing against Japhy's back in time with his footsteps (*Oh, honey I need you*) was our rucksack, and all we had left of home: clothes, the *Dove* album by James Lee Stanley, *The Dharma Bums* by Jack Kerouac, and Japhy's acoustic, which twang-thumped against my back with every step. We'd given up everything, said goodbye to everything, all because some fat politician had shoved his hand into a glass container where his sausage fingers death-gripped a blue plastic ball with *SEP 14* painted on it.

The song in my mind was silenced by a car engine buzzing in my ear like the drone of a hovering insect. I turned and saw its shiny carapace, a shimmering phantom on the horizon.

'Your turn,' I said.

Japhy squinted at the nearing vehicle, the sunlight reflecting off it in dazzling splinters of gold. 'Uh… dove.'

As the car drew near, we held out our thumbs and watched the shiny Mustang convertible with a grey-haired suit-and-tie-wearing-businessman at the wheel blur past.

'Aha! Hawk!' I grinned.

'Ray, just because he wore a suit and drove a fancy car, doesn't make him pro-war,' said Japhy. 'You can't judge people based on their physical appearances or possessions.'

'Oh, blah, blah. He seemed like part of the Establishment to me. And stop trying to weasel your way out of it! The only reason you don't like this game is because you're losing, babe. Another point to me.'

'Maybe we should get off these back roads?' said Japhy, staring first in one direction along the empty highway, and then in the other. 'No one's going to pick us up out here.'

'Maybe not,' I said. 'But that also means no one is gonna catch us, either. Come on.'

There's a rhythm to walking, much like music. Once you find it and hear the four-four beat inside your head (crunch, crunch, crunch, crunch) nothing else matters. Not the burn of your calves, not the ache of your feet, not the stink of your sweat. We'd become true Dharma Bums: sleeping on the ground, pissing in the grass, fucking under the stars, needing nothing else in the world but each other. I could walk for a thousand years as long as I had Japhy's shadow beside mine in the dirt.

'A lonely highway,' said Japhy. 'Sunlight blinds... from a windscreen.'

'Nice.' I nodded at his Kerouacian haiku: a flash in the mind, a glimpse at enlightenment, no rules, no form, just what-the-hell-ever man.

At the sound of another car, we held out our thumbs again.

'Dove,' said Japhy.

'It's not your turn!'

'Okay, fine, you call it then.' He raised eyebrow. A challenge.

I raised both eyebrows back at him. 'Hawk.'

The car was one of those ugly station wagons with fake wood paneling, and it slowed and then stopped ahead of us, its engine grumbling like a hungry stomach. I shook off my surprise, ran up to the car and grinned inside at three frat boys. They all looked alike: sky blue eyes complete with grey clouds, shark-white teeth in healthy gums, and chips on their shoulders bigger than their feet.

Biceps bulged the sleeves of their blue and yellow letter jackets, similar to those worn at Berkeley. I took a breath against images of green lawns, and student-filled commons, and sorority houses. Images I would never see for myself. Not now. My acceptance letter for California University – which I'd kept beneath my pillow to enhance my dreams – was in a crumpled up ball in my waste paper basket. Beside Japhy's crumpled draft notice and my crumpled hopes.

It wasn't fair.

For weeks, a hot balloon of pride and accomplishment had inflated inside my ribcage and kept my feet off the ground. We were going to Berkeley. Berkeley Fucking University! Just like Jack Kerouac. I was going to *be* somebody. I was going to *make something* of my life. And wouldn't that just shock the shit out of my folks.

And then, in a glinting, sharp-as-a-pin instant, my dreams had burst and I was left with an empty cavity where that balloon of pride had swelled.

But, giving all that up had been my choice. I'd convinced Japhy to drop everything and go to Canada. I'd convinced him Berkeley wasn't that important to me. I'd convinced him I had no regrets.

'Hey, man, thanks for stopping.' Japhy leaned down to

the window and smiled in at the driver. 'You're a lifesaver! A real lifesaver.'

And with his words, a little of my emptiness closed over. With his smile, a little of my icy regret thawed.

'Our pleasure.' The driver's words popped free from his chewing gum, and his oily gaze slid down my body and back up again.

'Three new strangers,' I mumbled to Japhy, 'give relief... to my sore feet.'

The backseat was littered with scrunched up crisp packets, chocolate-smeared candy-bar wrappers and empty beer bottles, which the frat in the back cleared with one arcing sweep of his giant arm. Japhy and I crawled in beside him, pushing our rucksack and guitar over the back onto their pile of bags. Before we could sit down properly, we slammed into our seats as the car rocketed back onto the road.

From the radio, the familiar four-four beat of James Lee Stanley's introduction began, and I grinned and leaned into Japhy, tapping my foot and nodding my head. It was a sign. A sign that everything would be fine now.

'Well I don't need no mighty mountain shining silver in the sun...'

'Hate this song!' The frat behind the wheel – the one with hair longer than the others, almost curly – leaned over and clicked the knob.

'Hey!' I sat up. 'I was listening to that.'

Curly Hair laughed, shrugged, and stared at the road ahead.

'I'm starving!' groaned the frat beside me. 'Can we stop soon and get some beers?' Two huge front teeth collided with his words, which hobbled from his mouth in an injured lisp.

'You're hungry for *beer*?' I snapped.

'We've got some wine in our bag, if you'd like some,' said Japhy, spinning around and reaching for our pack. He pulled out the half-empty stoppered bottle of red, as well as the cheese and bread we'd bought three days ago in Nashville before the long, foot-aching walk that had gotten us to this point.

Buckteeth snatched the cheese, bread and wine from Japhy, handed it through to the freckle-faced frat in the front passenger seat, who broke the food into three pieces and dispersed it all evenly between them, before tossing the empty bottle back to us.

I clenched my fists and opened my mouth to call them all selfish pigs, when I felt Japhy's hot breath whispering Kerouac into my ear: 'Practice charity without holding in mind any conceptions about charity, for charity after all is just a word.' He put his arm around me and pulled me against him, as if physically restraining me would cool the burning in my throat where volcanic words bubbled. 'So, where're you cats headed?' he asked.

'Road trip,' said Freckles. 'Last taste of freedom for a while.'

Buck Teeth turned to us. 'Start our army training in a few days.'

My eyes bulged and my jaw dropped. 'But, you don't have to enlist, and you won't be drafted; you're students.'

'We *were* students.' Buck Teeth grinned. 'Now, we're *soldiers!*'

All three frats started barking and grunting like a pack of wild animals.

'You're actually going Over There of your own free will to kill innocent people?' I lurched out of Japhy's hold and the dam of boiling word-lava broke. 'What the hell have they ever done to you?'

'Innocent?' Buck Teeth laughed. 'Don't you watch the news? Those Gooks ain't innocent!'

'Everyone's innocent to some degree!' I said. 'They're just as innocent as our side are!'

'North Vietnam are nothing but communist bullies!' said Buck Teeth. 'If we don't make a stand against them, and help defend South Vietnam, *our* country could be taken over by communism as well. You should be *thanking* us! We are fighting for *your* freedom!'

I crossed my arms. 'Oh, don't give me that line. Fighting for freedom! It's bullshit! It's the biggest oxymoron there is. People are *dying* and you are *defending* it!'

'Yes, I'm defending it,' said Buck Teeth. 'I think this war is good, but not because people are dying over there. It's good because we are helping other people to *live.*'

'That's the most ridiculous thing I've ever heard!' I said.

Japhy put his hand on my knee. 'Ray, come on, chill out, huh?'

'No, Japhy, it's a free country, I have a right to say how I feel. War is stupid and pointless, and anyone who believes it's *not* stupid, is stupid, too! No wonder the world is so screwed up with these idiot-sticks running around!'

Buck Teeth leaned past me to look at Japhy. 'Hey, you'd better tell your girlfriend to shut her mouth.'

'Excuse me!' I said, spinning around to face him. 'You can't tell me what to do. The only reason you don't want to hear my opinion is because you know I'm right. You feel guilty because the Establishment forced you into doing something you don't want to do!'

'Ray...' Japhy groaned.

'They aren't *forcing* us!' Buck Teeth said.

I wiped his spittle off my cheek and fired straight back at him. 'Bullshit! You are scared shitless of being drafted, so by joining of you own choice you've tricked yourselves into thinking what you're doing is right, even though you know it's not!'

'No, that's not–'

'There's no way you'd have the balls to do what Japhy is doing!'

'But, I–'

'He has been drafted, but instead of selling his soul to Nixon and compromising his beliefs, as you have done...'

'No we–'

'He is going to Canada!'

In the rear-vision mirror, Curly Hair's eyes narrowed at Japhy. 'You're a draft resister, huh?'

'You're damn right he is!' I smirked back at the driver's reflection.

And then I slammed into Japhy as the car made a fast, sharp turn off the highway onto a dirt road. He cried out as his head hit the window. Glass bottles clinked at our feet. The surrounding trees became so dense that only thin trickles of sunlight filtered through the canopy of branches above. The sky had turned its back on us.

'Why have we turned off the highway?' asked Japhy, rubbing his head.

'Shortcut,' muttered Curly Hair.

'You know the *one* thing I like about you long-hairs?' Buck Teeth lisped, his voice acquiring new strength. He put his hand on my knee, and began moving it up my thigh. 'The chicks always put-out.'

I slapped his hand away. 'Not with you, honey.'

'Hey, man, what is this?' Japhy asked.

'What this is, *man*, is something that don't concern you. So back off,' said Freckles.

The car rolled to a stop in a sunlit clearing as bright as the fear in Japhy's eyes.

And all three frat boys turned to face me.

***

Please visit www.mhsalter.com to download a free
excerpt, or to purchase this book.

a rose by any other name

❧

Chapter One

The Parkers

In the center of the room, a table. In the center of the table, a crystal ball. In the center of the crystal ball, Rose Parker's destiny waited to be revealed. It swirled and plinked against the glass, like a moth against a window, eager to break free and influence the future of the young woman to whom it was attached.

Above Rose Parker's head, smoke from spicy, eastern-flavored incense swirled in vortexes like entrances to other dimensions. Shadows from candle-flames flickered across the velvet walls and entered every bead in the curtained doorway; each tiny glass orb shone as bright as a promise.

Behind these strings of flame-encompassed beads, the

wisps and curls of smoke condensed together forming the tangible silhouette of a woman. Six feet tall, and curvaceously solid, her form possessed a fragile gracefulness despite her size. She floated forward through the clinking beads and into the candlelight, which revealed beautiful black hair and bright orange eyes.

With shaking hands, and a pounding heart, Rose wondered if she'd done the right thing by entering this tent. What if her play turned out to be a tragedy instead of a comedy? What if a misfortunate and piteous ending was written into her fifth act?

But her path led her into this tent for a reason, and after all, who was she to question the grand plan of Fate? Nobody. Just Rose Cordelia Parker. Just a lonely soul.

'Have a seat, child.' The gypsy's voice was soft and husky like rubber soles on gravel.

Rose sat and placed her hands on the table, palms flat down, fingers spread.

'Welcome,' said the gypsy, gliding onto the chair opposite. 'My name is Mab.'

'I'm Rose.'

'Twenty dollars, please, Rose.'

Rose slid the cash across the table and Mab picked up the money and stuffed it down the front of her dress. She cupped her hands around the crystal ball and her eyes glazed. 'Interesting.'

'What? What's interesting?' Rose leaned forward, squinting into the cold glass orb. All she could see was her distorted reflection staring back from the curve of the crystal sphere: her head enormous on a needle thin neck, skin as pale as her bleached blonde hair, and owl-wide eyes as black as the mysteries she was about to learn.

'There is a prophecy here,' whispered Mab. 'You carry it with you.'

'I carry a prophecy?'

'Yes, child. An age-old spite will once again be rife among those who've branched from the first quarrel. The streets will flow with crimson's tide of life, and stain the hands, and minds, of those moral. From each side of this battlefield romance will bloom between you and one forbidden. Your love will break the spell of hatred's trance, and uncover a secret long hidden. Bitterness dissolved, and old wounds healed, this peace will come at a grave and mortal price: two deaths. This noble bargain will be sealed. Hatred buried by love's self-sacrifice.'

'Huh?'

Mab looked up from the crystal ball and her amber eyes blazed. 'Love conquers all; a proverb that's on cue, for you may prove this old adage is true.'

Rose was silent.

'Your family is trapped within a curse of anger and vengeance, my dear; you and one other have the power to break this curse once and for all.'

Rose swallowed. She knew to what this must be referring. Her parents had been fighting with the Carlisles for as long as she could remember. But to be able to put a stop to it, to be able to live harmoniously in this town alongside Mr. and Mrs. Carlisle... Well, imagine that. Peace! It was something she would gladly fight for.

'What sort of power do I have?' croaked Rose.

'The most powerful weapon that we, as humans, possess.' Mab smiled. 'Love! Both the ability to love others, and the ability to have others love us in return.'

'And... the self-sacrifice thing?'

Mab's smile faltered, then faded altogether. 'Just because you are prophesized to end this hatred, does not mean you will survive it.' She reached across the table and grasped Rose's shaking hands tightly in thin, cold fingers.

'What are you saying?' asked Rose, squinting once again into the depths of the crystal ball.

'Do you believe in Fate, Rose? Do you believe that the paths of our future have already been laid for us?'

Rose nodded.

'Then I suggest you start looking for a way to change your path. Start looking before it is too late. I have foreseen your death, child, and it is not far away. However, our futures are simply the destinations of our present direction. But these directions *can* be changed, and therefore, so can our destinations.'

Rose wrenched her hands from the gypsy woman, wiping her palms on her shirt. As she bolted up, her chair thudded to the sawdust-strewn floor behind her, and her hip bumped against the table, rocking it on its foundations. The crystal ball rolled toward the edge, paused and then fell.

Rose prayed the ball would crack open when it hit the floor, and the prophecy would be freed, liberating her of the fate Mab had prophesized. But whether the glass smashed or not, Rose did not wait to find out.

The Carlisles

Ben Carlisle tightened his hands until they cramped: one on the wheel, one on the gearshift. His foot rested on the accelerator. A cold bead of sweat dribbled over the hill of his top lip into his mouth, and the saltiness made him think of blood. The throbbing in his ears increased in tempo as his heart counted off the seconds.

One, what am I doing? Two, what am I doing? Three, what am I doing?

How did he get here? Perched on a lookout facing a cliff, toward which he was about to drive as fast as he could, refusing to stop unless Claude Parker – who sat revving the car beside him – stopped first. Did he really think he could beat Claude at chicken? No one had *ever* beaten Claude at chicken. It was a wonder he hadn't gone over the edge in pure stubborn refusal to lose.

Four, what am I doing? Five, what am I doing?

This game was so stupid! It wasn't as if the winner won something substantial and worth risking their life for, like the other opponent's car for example. The simple acknowledgement of being the winner was the prize! To people like Claude Parker, however, that acknowledgement was the most important thing in the world. Being unbeaten. Being number one.

Ben's fingers crunched tighter around the steering wheel.

This game was stupid, but, he admitted, he would love to be the one to knock that jerk off his perch.

Ben allowed his eyes to snap to the side; he could see Claude – his eyes soft, his arm draped out the window, his smile wide – and something in that grin frightened the hell out of him. Claude was *relaxed*! As if he had accepted the possibility of death. Claude never lost this challenge, Ben realized, because he didn't care if he went over.

Ben took a shaky breath. *There is no way I can win. I am about to lose, or die.*

And all because I tried to stop this very thing from happening...

Just minutes ago, while driving through town, Ben had come to a set of green lights where two delivery trucks – a red Parker Estate van and a white Carlisle Wines van waited, stationary, ignoring the green lights, their engines revving.

'Not again,' Ben had groaned, stopping behind the two vans, and willing them to drive on. But they stayed stubbornly still.

Voices yelled in the front seats.

Ben sighed.

Praying no traffic was coming in the opposite direction, he swore under his breath and sped his red Torana out into the oncoming lane to draw level with the two vans.

'Stop this!' he had yelled loud enough so all four employees heard through the connecting tunnels of the three aligned front seats. 'You don't know what you're doing!'

And then suddenly, before he'd had a proper chance to break up this fight, another began.

A fourth car – a white Valiant – had revved to a stop beside Ben.

Now, all four lanes of the road were blocked.

Claude Parker's ice-blue eyes had glinted beneath the lowered curtains of his lids. His arm, sleeved in tattoos, rested on the lip of the open window. His white-blond hair, sharp with gel, flicked back and forward in the breeze.

'Don't tell me you're about to race the *workers*, Benny-Boy?' Claude yelled. 'In those cars?' He laughed and revved his engine. 'Take *me* on, instead. Make it worthy.'

Ben had held up his hands in a gesture of truce. 'Hey, I'm only trying to keep the peace, Claude. Either help me put a stop to these pathetic games, or piss off!'

'What?' Claude's mouth had drawn wide in a skullish grin. 'You're telling me you want *peace*? Peace!' He spat out his window; the green-tinged glob splatted heavily on the road. 'I hate that word just as much as I hate hell, all

Carlisles… and you!' He shook his head. 'You could never beat me, anyway. You don't have the balls. You're making excuses, Carlisle!'

'I'm not racing you, Parker!' shouted Ben.

Claude raised an eyebrow and stared at the road ahead as the silver gleam of a bumper on the horizon drew closer with every second. 'You know the rules, Ben. You get challenged: you race. Or the whole town hears about how gutless you are. About how all Carlisles are gutless!'

The oncoming vehicle drew closer still.

'No!' said Ben.

'Then I win, and your family's name stays in the mud, where it belongs.'

'No,' Ben had said again.

The green light turned amber and the silver car slowed as it approached and then pulled onto the shoulder to watch.

Claude punched his steering wheel. 'Race me, you chickenshit!'

Ben's heart banged its head against his ribcage. *I'm so sick of this bully thinking he's better and tougher than everyone. Someone needs to put him in his place.*

Claude's engine screamed with anticipation and Ben realized he no longer had a choice.

'First one to the lookout,' said Ben.

And Claude smiled. 'Last one to stop!'

On Ben's left, the two vans revved their engines. To his right, the guttural growl of Claude's car.

He sighed and placed his hand on the gearshift as the amber traffic light blinked up into red.

All four cars jerked forward. Gathered speed. Stayed level for a second or two. Then the vans dropped behind, leaving Ben and Claude – two streaks of red and white – speeding up the wrong side of the road.

As the vans shrank in his rear-view mirror, Ben imagined all those precious cases of wine in the cargo space, cracking together and bleeding out all over the floor. And he knew that even when the drivers returned to the vineyard with ruined cargo, his father would be *proud* that his loyal workers had defended the Carlisle name.

Two cars appeared directly ahead, driving straight at them and Ben's heart squeezed into his throat and he couldn't breathe as he swerved back into the correct lane too sharply and in a single blink of sweat from his eyes he was heading for the ditch on the side of the road.

Driven by fear and adrenaline, Ben jerked the wheel back onto the road with too much force and the car went into a 360 spin. The world outside cartwheeled around him. The side window jumped inward and smacked him on the forehead. The tires spun, screamed, smoked. But then the spiraling stopped. The road was ahead of him again. He was still racing. And Claude was beating him.

Ben reached the lookout a breath behind Claude.

He lined his car up even with Claude's, and stared

straight ahead at the 50 meters of road, and the eternity of nothing beyond it.

The white and red delivery vans arrived and parked off to the side, where the view was best. Then slowly, more cars, more spectators, appeared. Drawn solely by the tension in the air.

And they had waited...

And waited...

And now, here he still was, crouched over the wheel in concentration, about to drive full speed toward the edge of a cliff, below which was a drop of over 100 feet with razor sharp rocks and a hungry ocean. Why? Just to prove a stupid point to a stupid guy that he didn't care about anyway!

Ben heard the pounding surf even over the engine. It was angry today. And Ben wondered what his father would say tonight, when he found out about this.

Blood throbbed in his ears, counting off the seconds.

Ten, what am I doing? Eleven...

He would not move until Claude's tires spun first; this was the first challenge, seeing who would cave to the pressure. He might be able to at least win *this* part. Claude had lasted two whole hours once, before his opponent had mistaken the revving of a motorcycle for Claude's car, and leapt forward, beginning the second challenge.

Maybe my car will run out of petrol by then, and I won't have to go through with this ridiculous competition.

Seconds became minutes. Each car remained at the

starting point. More and more people gathered, forming two distinct sides, cheering and beeping their horns in excitement and impatience.

Suddenly Ben's car door was ripped open and his father's face grimaced down at him. The shock almost made Ben slam the car into gear and fly toward the cliff edge.

'Benedick Carlisle, what the *hell* are you doing?' Morgan Carlisle ripped the keys from the ignition. 'Get out here, right now.'

There was a groaning and booing from the crowd as Ben cringed out of the car, and stood staring at his feet in front of his pale, glaring parents.

'Hey, Carlisle!'

Looking out from under his shock of black hair, Ben saw Claude's parents, Shepherd and Imogen Parker, stomping toward them. Morgan Carlisle bristled and straightened to his full height.

Ben's mother, Desdemona, straightened as well. 'Go easy on them, Morgan!' she hissed, although the fierce flashing of her dark eyes belied her request.

To see the Parkers and the Carlisles standing side by side was to witness the true example of contrast. The Parkers were white-blond with bright blue eyes, and smooth milky skin. The Carlisles: olive-skinned, hair like ebony, and eyes like black diamonds. All four stood, eyes bulging with hatred at each other.

'Your bloody son is a menace!' Morgan Carlisle

stabbed a shaking finger at Claude, who gleamed behind his parents. 'Organizing these idiotic races!'

'*My* son?' Shepherd Parker, white with anger, ripped his arm away from his wife, who tried unsuccessfully to hold him back. 'Claude says *Ben* gave out the challenge!'

Morgan stormed toward Shepherd, his fists balled at his sides, his face red and his dark eyes wide and fierce. But Desdemona stepped in front of her husband, pushing against his chest, and shaking her head. Her black hair blew wild about her face, snapping in the wind.

'Move, Des!' Morgan growled.

'You will *not* take one more step toward him, Morgan Carlisle. You will *not* start a fight in the middle of all these witnesses!'

When the whoop-whoop of a siren sliced through the tension-thick air, the group of onlookers parted down the middle. A police car slid through them into the lookout; a stroboscopic disco of blue and red flashed over every eager face.

Ben groaned as he recognized the stocky body, closely cropped hair, squashed nose and loose jowls of police sergeant, Henry Burgundy.

The officer stepped out of the car and rose to his full height. 'You two will not learn!' He stared down at Shepherd Parker and then Morgan Carlisle. 'You won't be satisfied until this fire is quenched by your own blood.' Burgundy turned and gestured toward Ben. 'Or your *children's* blood! You hurt, son?'

'Wha... No, sir.' Ben shrugged.

Burgundy pulled a white handkerchief from his breast pocket and handed it to Ben, who took it and stared at the clean square of cotton.

'For your head, son.' Burgundy said.

Ben scrunched the handkerchief and wiped it across his forehead, expecting it to soak up his nervous sweat. Instead, its clean whiteness stained red. 'Oh.'

'This is the *third* time this week you have caused a disturbance!' Burgundy yelled at Morgan. 'I'm giving you one more chance.' He held up a stubby finger. '*One*. The very next person who disturbs the quiet of my streets will be arrested and sent straight to jail. No trial. No bail.' Back he turned to Shepherd Parker. 'You, Parker, follow me to the courthouse. Carlisle, come and see me this afternoon. We'll sort this out once and for all.'

Burgundy threw a glance at each of them, one by one, his piercing eyes lingering on them for an uncomfortable second, then he threw his words out to the gathered crowd. 'The rest of you: get out of here before I start handing out fines! And don't think I won't!'

Then he folded himself back into his cruiser and drove away.

'Come on, son.' Morgan put his arm around Ben and led him away from the Parkers and back to Ben's car. 'So, who *did* start it this time?'

'Not me!'

Morgan raised his eyebrows and looked at his wife.

'It *wasn't!*' Ben cleared his throat and looked down at his fidgeting hands. 'He called me a chickenshit.'

Morgan looked away, his eyes narrowing, and he grunted. Ben couldn't tell if it was a proud grunt at the refusal to back down to a Parker, or a frustrated grunt at the refusal to back down to a Parker.

'Oh, where's Topher?' sighed Desdemona, as she stared at the clouds beyond the cliff edge. 'Have you seen him today, Ben? I'm so glad he wasn't involved in all this.'

Ben's gut twinged at the mention of his brother, the golden boy, the favorite.

'I saw him earlier,' Ben answered, 'walking in that grove of trees at the edge of town. He looked like he wanted to be alone. I left him to it.'

Morgan nodded. 'He's been so depressed lately. He stays out all hours of the night, and then stumbles home, draws all the curtains and hides. It's not healthy.'

'What's his problem this time?' Ben asked.

'He won't talk to anyone!' sighed Morgan.

As if drawn by the mere mention of his beloved name, Topher Carlisle sped past the lookout in his bright green Holden Belmont, heading into town.

'Leave it to me.' Ben plucked his keys back from his father's hand.

So, poor depressed Topher has a secret, does he? Well, not for long.

***

Please visit www.mhsalter.com to download a free excerpt, or to purchase this book.

www.ingramcontent.com/pod-product-compliance
Lightning Source LLC
Chambersburg PA
CBHW020617120726
47905CB00003B/835